*Selected Stories by*
H. RIDER HAGGARD

## Books in this Series:

*Selected Stories by O. Henry*
*Selected Stories by Anton Chekhov*
*Selected Stories by Guy de Maupassant*
*Selected Stories by Mark Twain*
*Selected Stories by Edgar Allan Poe*
*Selected Stories by Rudyard Kipling*
*Selected Stories by Saki*
*Selected Stories by Oscar Wilde*
*Selected Stories by Honoré de Balzac*
*Selected Stories by Charles Dickens*
*Selected Stories by D.H. Lawrence*
*Selected Stories by H.G. Wells*
*Selected Stories by Jack London*
*Selected Stories by Joseph Conrad*
*Selected Stories by Leo Tolstoy*
*Selected Stories by Sir Arthur Conan Doyle*
*Selected Stories by James Joyce*
*Selected Stories by Virginia Woolf*
*Selected Stories by Thomas Hardy*
*Selected Stories by Fyodor Dostoyevsky*
*Selected Stories by Katherine Mansfield*
*Selected Stories by Wilkie Collins*
*Selected Stories by Robert Louis Stevenson*
*Selected Stories by Howard Pyle*
*Selected Stories by Jerome K. Jerome*
*Selected Stories by Sir Walter Scott*
*Selected Stories by G.K. Chesterton*

# *Selected Stories by*
# H. RIDER HAGGARD

Published by
Rupa Publications India Pvt. Ltd 2015
7/16, Ansari Road, Daryaganj
New Delhi 110002

*Sales centres:*
Allahabad Bengaluru Chennai
Hyderabad Jaipur Kathmandu
Kolkata Mumbai

Selection and Introduction copyright © Terry O'Brien 2015

All rights reserved.
No part of this publication may be reproduced, transmitted,
or stored in a retrieval system, in any form or by any means,
electronic, mechanical, photocopying, recording or otherwise,
without the prior permission of the publisher.

ISBN: 978-81-291-3688-6

First impression 2015

10 9 8 7 6 5 4 3 2 1

Printed at Shree Maitrey Printech Pvt. Ltd., Noida

This book is sold subject to the condition that it shall not,
by way of trade or otherwise, be lent, resold, hired out, or otherwise
circulated, without the publisher's prior consent, in any form of binding or
cover other than that in which it is published.

# CONTENTS

*Introduction*   vii

1. Long Odds   1
2. Little Flower   19
3. The Blue Curtains   93

# INTRODUCTION

Sir Henry Rider Haggard (22 June 1856–14 May 1925) was a prolific English writer of adventure stories and a pioneer of the Lost World literary genre. What makes his writing unique is the portrayal of Africa and its native people in most of his novels. His stories are easy to read and continue to attract readers of all age groups.

Haggard created Allan Quatermain, one of the greatest literary heroes of the British Victorian era, and gained immense popularity with the publication of *King Solomon's Mines* in 1885.

- 'Long Odds' is the story of Allan Quatermain or Hunter Quatermain and his encounter with a family of lions in the jungles of Africa.
- In 'Little Flower' an English missionary and his family come to live with the Zulu tribe in Africa to spread Christianity among the natives. Faced with opposition, the missionary challenges his adversary Menzi, a local witch-doctor with magical powers. From fantastic magical demonstrations to a brilliant finale, this fast-paced story will surely keep readers hooked!
- First published in 1886, 'The Blue Curtains' is the story of 'Bottles', a British army captain stationed in South Africa and his tragic love affair with a woman in London.

# 1

## LONG ODDS

The story which is narrated in the following pages came to me from the lips of my old friend Allan Quatermain, or Hunter Quatermain, as we used to call him in South Africa. He told it to me one evening when I was stopping with him at the place he bought in Yorkshire. Shortly after that, the death of his only son so unsettled him that he immediately left England, accompanied by two companions, his old fellow-voyagers, Sir Henry Curtis and Captain Good, and has now utterly vanished into the dark heart of Africa. He is persuaded that a white people, of which he has heard rumours all his life, exists somewhere on the highlands in the vast, still unexplored interior, and his great ambition is to find them before he dies. This is the wild quest upon which he and his companions have departed, and from which I shrewdly suspect they never will return. One letter only have I received from the old gentleman, dated from a mission station high up the Tana, a river on the east coast, about three hundred miles north of Zanzibar. In it he says that they have gone through many hardships and adventures, but are alive and well, and have found traces which go far towards making him hope that the results of their wild quest may be a 'magnificent and unexampled discovery'. I greatly fear, however, that all he has discovered is death; for this letter came a long while ago, and nobody has heard a single word of the party since. They have totally vanished.

It was on the last evening of my stay at his house that he told the ensuing story to me and Captain Good, who was dining with him. He had eaten his dinner and drunk two or three glasses of old port, just to help Good and myself to the end of the second bottle. It was an unusual thing for him to do, for he was a most abstemious man, having conceived, as he used to say, a great horror of drink from observing its effects upon the class of colonists—hunters, transport riders and others—amongst whom he had passed so many years of his life. Consequently the good wine took more effect on him than it would have done on most men, sending a little flush into his wrinkled cheeks, and making him talk more freely than usual.

Dear old man! I can see him now, as he went limping up and down the vestibule, with his grey hair sticking up in scrubbing-brush fashion, his shrivelled yellow face, and his large dark eyes, that were as keen as any hawk's, and yet soft as a buck's. The whole room was hung with trophies of his numerous hunting expeditions, and he had some story about every one of them, if only he could be got to tell it. Generally he would not, for he was not very fond of narrating his own adventures, but to-night the port wine made him more communicative.

'Ah, you brute!' he said, stopping beneath an unusually large skull of a lion, which was fixed just over the mantelpiece, beneath a long row of guns, its jaws distended to their utmost width. 'Ah, you brute! you have given me a lot of trouble for the last dozen years, and will, I suppose to my dying day.'

'Tell us the yarn, Quatermain,' said Good. 'You have often promised to tell me, and you never have.'

'You had better not ask me to,' he answered, 'for it is a longish one.'

'All right,' I said, 'the evening is young, and there is some more port.'

Thus adjured, he filled his pipe from a jar of coarse-cut Boer tobacco that was always standing on the mantelpiece, and still walking up and down the room, began—

'It was, I think, in the March of '69 that I was up in Sikukuni's country. It was just after old Sequati's time, and Sikukuni had got into power—I forget how. Anyway, I was there. I had heard that the Bapedi people had brought down an enormous quantity of ivory from the interior, and so I started with a waggon-load of goods, and came straight away from Middelburg to try and trade some of it. It was a risky thing to go into the country so early, on account of the fever; but I knew that there were one or two others after that lot of ivory, so I determined to have a try for it, and take my chance of fever. I had become so tough from continual knocking about that I did not set it down at much.

'Well, I got on all right for a while. It is a wonderfully beautiful piece of bush veldt, with great ranges of mountains running through it, and round granite koppies starting up here and there, looking out like sentinels over the rolling waste of bush. But it is very hot—hot as a stew-pan—and when I was there that March, which, of course, is autumn in this part of Africa, the whole place reeked of fever. Every morning, as I trekked along down by the Oliphant River, I used to creep from the waggon at dawn and look out. But there was no river to be seen—only a long line of billows of what looked like the finest cotton wool tossed up lightly with a pitchfork. It was the fever miSt Out from among the scrub, too, came little spirals of vapour, as though there were hundreds of tiny fires alight in it—reek rising from thousands of tons of rotting vegetation. It was a beautiful place, but the beauty was the beauty of death; and all those lines and blots of vapour wrote one great word across the surface of the country, and that word was "fever."

'It was a dreadful year of illness that. I came, I remember, to one little kraal of Knobnoses, and went up to it to see if I could get some "maas", or curdled butter-milk, and a few mealies. As I drew near I was struck with the silence of the place. No children began to chatter, and no dogs barked. Nor could I see any native sheep or cattle. The place, though it had evidently been inhabited of late, was as still as the bush round it, and some guinea-fowl got up out of the prickly pear bushes right at the kraal gate. I remember that I hesitated a little before going in, there was such an air of desolation about the spot. Nature never looks desolate when man has not yet laid his hand upon her breast; she is only lonely. But when man has been, and has passed away, then she looks desolate.

'Well, I passed into the kraal, and went up to the principal hut. In front of the hut was something with an old sheep-skin kaross thrown over it. I stooped down and drew off the rug, and then shrank back amazed, for under it was the body of a young woman recently dead. For a moment I thought of turning back, but my curiosity overcame me; so going past the dead woman, I went down on my hands and knees and crept into the hut. It was so dark that I could not see anything, though I could smell a great deal, so I lit a match. It was a "tandstickor" match, and burnt slowly and dimly, and as the light gradually increased I made out what I took to be a family of people, men, women and children, fast asleep. Presently it burnt up brightly, and I saw that they too, five of them altogether, were quite dead. One was a baby. I dropped the match in a hurry, and was making my way from the hut as quick as I could go, when I caught sight of two bright eyes staring out of a corner. Thinking it was a wild cat, or some such animal, I redoubled my haste, when suddenly a voice near the eyes began first to mutter, and then to send up a succession of awful yells.

'Hastily I lit another match, and perceived that the eyes belonged to an old woman, wrapped up in a greasy leather garment. Taking her by the arm, I dragged her out, for she could not, or would not, come by herself, and the stench was overpowering me. Such a sight as she was—a bag of bones, covered over with black, shrivelled parchment. The only white thing about her was her wool, and she seemed to be pretty well dead except for her eyes and her voice. She thought that I was a devil come to take her, and that is why she yelled so. Well, I got her down to the waggon, and gave her a "tot" of Cape smoke, and then, as soon as it was ready, poured about a pint of beef-tea down her throat, made from the flesh of a blue vilderbeeste I had killed the day before, and after that she brightened up wonderfully. She could talk Zulu—indeed, it turned out that she had run away from Zululand in T'Chaka's time—and she told me that all the people whom I had seen had died of fever. When they had died the other inhabitants of the kraal had taken the cattle and gone away, leaving the poor old woman, who was helpless from age and infirmity, to perish of starvation or disease, as the case might be. She had been sitting there for three days among the bodies when I found her. I took her on to the next kraal, and gave the headman a blanket to look after her, promising him another if I found her well when I came back. I remember that he was much astonished at my parting with two blankets for the sake of such a worthless old creature. "Why did I not leave her in the bush?" he asked. Those people carry the doctrine of the survival of the fittest to its extreme, you see.

'It was the night after I had got rid of the old woman that I made my first acquaintance with my friend yonder,' and he nodded towards the skull that seemed to be grinning down at us in the shadow of the wide mantelshelf. 'I had trekked from dawn till eleven o'clock—a long trek—but I wanted to get on, and had turned the oxen out to graze, sending the voorlooper to look after them, my intention being to inspan again about six o'clock, and trek with the moon till ten. Then I got into the waggon and had a good sleep till half-past two or so in the afternoon, when I rose and cooked some meat, and had my dinner, washing it down with a pannikin of black coffee—for it was difficult to get preserved milk in those days. Just as I had finished, and the driver, a man called Tom, was washing up the things, in comes the young scoundrel of a voorlooper driving one ox before him.

"'Where are the other oxen?' I asked.

"'Koos!' he said, 'Koos! the other oxen have gone away. I turned my back for a minute, and when I looked round again they were all gone except Kaptein, here, who was rubbing his back against a tree.'

"'You mean that you have been asleep, and let them stray, you villain. I will rub your back against a stick,' I answered, feeling very angry, for it was not a pleasant prospect to be stuck up in that fever trap for a week or so while we were hunting for the oxen. 'Off you go, and you too, Tom, and mind you don't come back till you have found them. They have trekked back along the Middelburg Road, and are a dozen miles off by now, I'll be bound. Now, no words; go both of you.'

'Tom, the driver, swore, and caught the lad a hearty kick, which he richly deserved, and then, having tied old Kaptein up to the disselboom with a reim, they took their assegais and sticks, and started. I would have gone too, only I knew that somebody must look after the waggon, and I did not like to leave either of the boys with it at night. I was in a very bad temper, indeed, although I was pretty well used to these sort of occurrences, and soothed myself by taking a rifle and going to kill something. For a couple of hours I poked about without seeing anything that I could get a shot at, but at last, just as

I was again within seventy yards of the waggon, I put up an old Impala ram from behind a mimosa thorn. He ran straight for the waggon, and it was not till he was passing within a few feet of it that I could get a decent shot at him. Then I pulled, and caught him half-way down the spine. Over he went, dead as a door-nail, and a pretty shot it was, though I ought not to say it. This little incident put me into rather a better humour, especially as the buck had rolled right against the after-part of the waggon, so I had only to gut him, fix a reim round his legs, and haul him up. By the time I had done this the sun was down, and the full moon was up, and a beautiful moon it was. And then there came that wonderful hush which sometimes falls over the African bush in the early hours of the night. No beast was moving, and no bird called. Not a breath of air stirred the quiet trees, and the shadows did not even quiver, they only grew. It was very oppressive and very lonely, for there was not a sign of the cattle or the boys. I was quite thankful for the society of old Kaptein, who was lying down contentedly against the disselboom, chewing the cud with a good conscience.

'Presently, however, Kaptein began to get restless. First he snorted, then he got up and snorted again. I could not make it out, so like a fool I got down off the waggon-box to have a look round, thinking it might be the lost oxen coming.

'Next instant I regretted it, for all of a sudden I heard a roar and saw something yellow flash past me and light on poor Kaptein. Then came a bellow of agony from the ox, and a crunch as the lion put his teeth through the poor brute's neck, and I began to understand what had happened. My rifle was in the waggon, and my first thought being to get hold of it, I turned and made a bolt for the box. I got my foot up on the wheel and flung my body forward on to the waggon, and there I stopped as if I were frozen, and no wonder, for as I was about to spring up I heard the lion behind me, and next second I felt the brute, ay, as plainly as I can feel this table. I felt him, I say, sniffing at my left leg that was hanging down.

'My word! I did feel queer; I don't think that I ever felt so queer before. I dared not move for the life of me, and the odd thing was that I seemed to lose power over my leg, which developed an insane sort of inclination to kick out of its own mere motion—just as hysterical people want to laugh when they ought to be particularly solemn. Well, the lion sniffed and sniffed, beginning at my ankle and slowly nosing away up to my thigh. I thought that he was going to get hold then, but he did not. He only growled softly, and went back to the ox. Shifting my head a little I got a full view of him. He was about the biggest lion I ever saw, and I have seen a great many, and he had a most tremendous black mane. What his teeth were like you can see—look there, pretty big ones, ain't they? Altogether he was a magnificent animal, and as I lay sprawling on the fore-tongue of the waggon, it occurred to me that he would look uncommonly well in a cage. He stood there by the carcass of poor Kaptein, and deliberately disembowelled him as neatly as a butcher could have done. All this while I dared not move, for he kept lifting his head and keeping an eye on me as he licked his bloody chops. When he had cleaned Kaptein out he opened his mouth and roared, and I am not exaggerating when I say that the sound shook the waggon. Instantly there came back an answering roar.

'"Heavens!" I thought, "there is his mate."

'Hardly was the thought out of my head when I caught sight in the moonlight of the lioness bounding along through the long grass, and after her a couple of cubs about the size of mastiffs. She stopped within a few feet of my head, and stood, waved her tail, and fixed me with her glowing yellow eyes; but just as I thought that it was all over she turned and began to feed on Kaptein, and so did the cubs. There were the four of them within eight feet of me, growling and quarrelling, rending and tearing, and crunching poor Kaptein's bones; and there I lay shaking with terror, and the cold perspiration pouring out of me, feeling like another Daniel come to judgment in a new sense of the phrase. Presently the cubs had eaten their fill, and began to get restless. One went round to the back of the waggon and pulled at the Impala buck that hung there, and the other came round my way and commenced the sniffing game at my leg. Indeed, he did more than that, for, my trouser being hitched up a little, he began to lick the bare skin with his rough tongue. The more he licked the more he liked it, to judge from his increased vigour and the loud purring noise he made. Then I knew that the end had come, for in another second his file-like tongue would have rasped through the skin of my leg—which was luckily pretty tough—and have drawn the blood, and then there would be no chance for me. So I just lay there and thought of my sins, and prayed to the Almighty, and reflected that after all life was a very enjoyable thing.

'Then all of a sudden I heard a crashing of bushes and the shouting and whistling of men, and there were the two boys coming back with the cattle, which they had found trekking along all together. The lions lifted their heads and listened, then bounded off without a sound—and I fainted.

'The lions came back no more that night, and by the next morning my nerves had got pretty straight again; but I was full of wrath when I thought of all that I had gone through at the hands, or rather noses, of those four brutes, and of the fate of my after-ox Kaptein. He was a splendid ox, and I was very fond of him. So wroth was I that like a fool I determined to attack the whole family of them. It was worthy of a greenhorn out on his first hunting trip; but I did it nevertheless. Accordingly after breakfast, having rubbed some oil upon my leg, which was very sore from the cub's tongue, I took the driver, Tom, who did not half like the business, and having armed myself with an ordinary double No. 12 smoothbore, the first breechloader I ever had, I started. I took the smoothbore because it shot a bullet very well; and my experience has been that a round ball from a smoothbore is quite as effective against a lion as an express bullet. The lion is soft, and not a difficult animal to finish if you hit him anywhere in the body. A buck takes far more killing.

'Well, I started, and the first thing I set to work to do was to try to discover whereabouts the brutes lay up for the day. About three hundred yards from the waggon was the crest of a rise covered with single mimosa trees, dotted about in a park-like fashion, and beyond this lay a stretch of open plain running down to a dry pan, or water-hole, which covered about an acre of ground, and was densely clothed with reeds, now in the sere and yellow leaf. From the further edge of this pan the ground sloped up again to a great cleft, or nullah, which had been cut out by the action of the water, and was pretty thickly sprinkled with bush, amongst which grew some large trees, I forget of what sort.

'It at once struck me that the dry pan would be a likely place to find my friends in, as there is nothing a lion is fonder of than lying up in reeds, through which he can see things without being seen himself. Accordingly thither I went and prospected. Before I had got half-way round the pan I found the remains of a blue vilderbeeste that had evidently been killed within the last three or four days and partially devoured by lions; and from other indications about I was soon assured that if the family were not in the pan that day they spent a good deal of their spare time there. But if there, the question was how to get them out; for it was clearly impossible to think of going in after them unless one was quite determined to commit suicide. Now there was a strong wind blowing from the direction of the waggon, across the reedy pan towards the bush-clad kloof or donga, and this first gave me the idea of firing the reeds, which, as I think I told you, were pretty dry. Accordingly Tom took some matches and began starting little fires to the left, and I did the same to the right. But the reeds were still green at the bottom, and we should never have got them well alight had it not been for the wind, which grew stronger and stronger as the sun climbed higher, and forced the fire into them. At last, after half-an-hour's trouble, the flames got a hold, and began to spread out like a fan, whereupon I went round to the further side of the pan to wait for the lions, standing well out in the open, as we stood at the copse to-day where you shot the woodcock. It was a rather risky thing to do, but I used to be so sure of my shooting in those days that I did not so much mind the risk. Scarcely had I got round when I heard the reeds parting before the onward rush of some animal. "Now for it," said I. On it came. I could see that it was yellow, and prepared for action, when instead of a lion out bounded a beautiful reit bok which had been lying in the shelter of the pan. It must, by the way, have been a reit bok of a peculiarly confiding nature to lay itself down with the lion, like the lamb of prophesy, but I suppose the reeds were thick, and that it kept a long way off.

'Well, I let the reit bok go, and it went like the wind, and kept my eyes fixed upon the reeds. The fire was burning like a furnace now; the flames crackling and roaring as they bit into the reeds, sending spouts of fire twenty feet and more into the air, and making the hot air dance above in a way that was perfectly dazzling. But the reeds were still half green, and created an enormous quantity of smoke, which came rolling towards me like a curtain, lying very low on account of the wind. Presently, above the crackling of the fire, I heard a startled roar, then another and another. So the lions were at home.

'I was beginning to get excited now, for, as you fellows

know, there is nothing in experience to warm up your nerves like a lion at close quarters, unless it is a wounded buffalo; and I became still more so when I made out through the smoke that the lions were all moving about on the extreme edge of the reeds. Occasionally they would pop their heads out like rabbits from a burrow, and then, catching sight of me standing about fifty yards away, draw them back again. I knew that it must be getting pretty warm behind them, and that they could not keep the game up for long; and I was not mistaken, for suddenly all four of them broke cover together, the old black-maned lion leading by a few yards. I never saw a more splendid sight in all my hunting experience than those four lions bounding across the veldt, overshadowed by the dense pall of smoke and backed by the fiery furnace of the burning reeds.

'I reckoned that they would pass, on their way to the bushy kloof, within about five and twenty yards of me, so, taking a long breath, I got my gun well on to the lion's shoulder—the black-maned one—so as to allow for an inch or two of motion, and catch him through the heart. I was on, dead on, and my finger was just beginning to tighten on the trigger, when suddenly I went blind—a bit of reed-ash had drifted into my right eye. I danced and rubbed, and succeeded in clearing it more or less just in time to see the tail of the last lion vanishing round the bushes up the kloof.

'If ever a man was mad I was that man. It was too bad; and such a shot in the open! However, I was not going to be beaten, so I just turned and marched for the kloof. Tom, the driver, begged and implored me not to go, but though as a general rule I never pretend to be very brave (which I am not), I was determined that I would either kill those lions or they should kill me. So I told Tom that he need not come unless he liked, but I was going; and being a plucky fellow, a Swazi by birth, he shrugged his shoulders, muttered that I was mad or bewitched, and followed doggedly in my tracks.

'We soon reached the kloof, which was about three hundred yards in length and but sparsely wooded, and then the real fun began. There might be a lion behind every bush—there certainly were four lions somewhere; the delicate question was, where. I peeped and poked and looked in every possible direction, with my heart in my mouth, and was at last rewarded by catching a glimpse of something yellow moving behind a bush. At the same moment, from another bush opposite me out burst one of the cubs and galloped back towards the burnt pan. I whipped round and let drive a snap shot that tipped him head over heels, breaking his back within two inches of the root of the tail, and there he lay helpless but glaring. Tom afterwards killed him with his assegai. I opened the breech of the gun and hurriedly pulled out the old case, which, to judge from what ensued, must, I suppose, have burst and left a portion of its fabric sticking to the barrel. At any rate, when I tried to get in the new cartridge it would only enter half-way; and—would you believe it?—this was the moment that the lioness, attracted no doubt by the outcry of her cub, chose to put in an appearance. There she stood, twenty paces or so from me, lashing her tail and looking just as wicked as it is possible to conceive. Slowly I stepped backwards, trying to push in the new case, and as I did so she moved on in little runs, dropping down after each run. The danger was imminent, and the case would not go in. At the moment I oddly enough thought of the cartridge maker, whose name I will not mention, and earnestly hoped that if the lion got *me* some condign punishment would overtake *him*. It would not go in, so I tried to pull it out. It would not come out either, and my gun was useless if I could not shut it to use the other barrel. I might as well have had no gun.

'Meanwhile I was walking backward, keeping my eye on the lioness, who was creeping forward on her belly without a sound, but lashing her tail and keeping her eye on me; and in it I saw that she was coming in a few seconds more. I dashed my wrist and the palm of my hand against the brass rim of the cartridge till the blood poured from them—look, there are the scars of it to this day!'

Here Quatermain held up his right hand to the light and showed us four or five white cicatrices just where the wrist is set into the hand.

'But it was not of the slightest use,' he went on, 'the cartridge would not move. I only hope that no other man will ever be put in such an awful position. The lioness gathered herself together, and I gave myself up for lost, when suddenly Tom shouted out from somewhere in my rear—

'"You are walking on to the wounded cub; turn to the right."

'I had the sense, dazed as I was, to take the hint, and slewing round at right-angles, but still keeping my eyes on the lioness, I continued my backward walk.

'To my intense relief, with a low growl she straightened herself, turned, and bounded further up the kloof.

'"Come on, Macumazahn," said Tom, "let's get back to the waggon."

'"All right, Tom," I answered. "I will when I have killed those three other lions," for by this time I was bent on shooting them as I never remember being bent on anything before or since. "You can go if you like, or you can get up a tree."

'He considered the position a little, and then he very wisely got up a tree. I wish that I had done the same.

'Meanwhile I had found my knife, which had an extractor in it, and succeeded after some difficulty in pulling out the cartridge which had so nearly been the cause of my death, and removing the obstruction in the barrel. It was very little thicker than a postage-stamp; certainly not thicker than a piece of writing-paper. This done, I loaded the gun, bound a handkerchief round my wrist and hand to staunch the flowing of the blood, and started on again.

'I had noticed that the lioness went into a thick green bush, or rather cluster of bushes, growing near the water, about fifty yards higher up, for there was a little stream running down the kloof, and I walked towards this bush. When I got there, however, I could see nothing, so I took up a big stone and threw it into the bushes. I believe that it hit the other cub, for out it came with a rush, giving me a broadside shot, of which I promptly availed myself, knocking it over dead. Out, too, came the lioness like a flash of light, but quick as she went I managed to put the other bullet into her ribs, so that she rolled right over three times like a shot rabbit. I instantly got two more cartridges into the gun, and as I did so the lioness rose again and came crawling towards me on her fore-paws, roaring and groaning, and with such an expression of diabolical fury on her countenance as I have not often seen. I shot her again through the chest, and she fell over on to her side quite dead.

'That was the first and last time that I ever killed a brace of lions right and left, and, what is more, I never heard of anybody else doing it. Naturally I was considerably pleased with myself, and having again loaded up, I went on to look for the black-maned beauty who had killed Kaptein. Slowly, and with the greatest care, I proceeded up the kloof, searching every bush and tuft of grass as I went. It was wonderfully exciting, work, for I never was sure from one moment to another but that he would be on me. I took comfort, however, from the reflection that a lion rarely attacks a man—rarely, I say; sometimes he does, as you will see—unless he is cornered or wounded. I must have been nearly an hour hunting after that lion. Once I thought I saw something move in a clump of tambouki grass, but I could not be sure, and when I trod out the grass I could not find him.

'At last I worked up to the head of the kloof, which made a cul-de-sac. It was formed of a wall of rock about fifty feet high. Down this rock trickled a little waterfall, and in front of it, some seventy feet from its face, rose a great piled-up mass of boulders, in the crevices and on the top of which grew ferns, grasses and stunted bushes. This mass was about twenty-five feet high. The sides of the kloof here were also very steep. Well, I came to the top of the nullah and looked all round. No signs of the lion. Evidently I had either overlooked him further down or he had escaped right away. It was very vexatious; but still three lions were not a bad bag for one gun before dinner, and I was fain to be content. Accordingly I departed back again, making my way round the isolated pillar of boulders, beginning to feel, as I did so, that I was pretty well done up with excitement and fatigue, and should be more so before I had skinned those three lions. When I had got, as nearly as I could judge, about eighteen yards past the pillar or mass of boulders, I turned to have another look round. I have a pretty sharp eye, but I could see nothing at all.

'Then, on a sudden, I saw something sufficiently alarming. On the top of the mass of boulders, opposite to me, standing out clear against the rock beyond, was the huge black-maned lion. He had been crouching there, and now arose as though by magic. There he stood lashing his tail, just like a living reproduction of the animal on the gateway of Northumberland House that I have seen in a picture. But he did not stand long. Before I could fire—before I could do more than get the gun to my shoulder—he sprang straight up and out from the rock, and driven by the impetus of that one mighty bound came hurtling through the air towards me.

'Heavens! how grand he looked, and how awful! High into the air he flew, describing a great arch. Just as he touched the highest point of his spring I fired. I did not dare to wait, for I saw that he would clear the whole space and land right upon me. Without a sight, almost without aim, I fired, as one would fire a snap shot at a snipe. The bullet told, for I distinctly heard its thud above the rushing sound caused by the passage of the lion through the air. Next second I was swept to the ground (luckily I fell into a low, creeper-clad bush, which broke the shock), and the lion was on the top of me, and the next those great white teeth of his had met in my thigh—I heard them grate against the bone. I yelled out in agony, for I did not feel in the least benumbed and happy, like Dr Livingstone—whom, by the way, I knew very well—and gave myself up for dead. But suddenly, at that moment, the lion's grip on my thigh loosened, and he stood over me, swaying to and fro, his huge mouth, from which the blood was gushing, wide opened. Then he roared, and the sound shook the rocks.

'To and fro he swung, and then the great head dropped on me, knocking all the breath from my body, and he was dead. My bullet had entered in the centre of his chest and passed out on the right side of the spine about half way down the back.

'The pain of my wound kept me from fainting, and as soon as I got my breath I managed to drag myself from under him. Thank heavens, his great teeth had not crushed my thigh-bone; but I was losing a great deal of blood, and had it not been for the timely arrival of Tom, with whose aid I loosed the handkerchief from my wrist and tied it round my leg, twisting it tight with a stick, I think that I should have bled to death.

'Well, it was a just reward for my folly in trying to tackle a family of lions single-handed. The odds were too long. I have been lame ever since, and shall be to my dying day; in the month of March the wound always troubles me a great deal, and every three years it breaks out raw.

'I need scarcely add that I never traded the lot of ivory at Sikukuni's. Another man got it—a German—and made five hundred pounds out of it after paying expenses. I spent the next month on the broad of my back, and was a cripple for six months after that. And now I've told you the yarn, so I will have a drop of Hollands and go to bed. Good-night to you all, good-night!'

# 2

# LITTLE FLOWER

I

The Rev. Thomas Bull was a man of rock-like character with no more imagination than a rock. Of good birth, good abilities, good principles and good repute, really he ought to have been named not Thomas but John Bull, being as he was a typical representative of the British middle class. By nature a really religious man and, owing to the balance of his mind, not subject to most of the weaknesses which often afflict others, very early in his career he determined that things spiritual were of far greater importance than things temporal, and that as Eternity is much longer than Time, it was wise to devote himself to the spiritual and leave the temporal to look after itself. There are quite a number of good people, earnest believers in the doctrine of rewards and punishments, who take that practical view. With such

'Repaid a thousand-fold shall be,'

is a favourite line of a favourite hymn.

It is true that his idea of the spiritual was limited. Perhaps it would be more accurate to say that it was unlimited, since he accepted without doubt or question everything that was to be found within the four corners of what he had been taught. As a boy he had been noted for his prowess in swallowing the largest pills.

'Don't think,' he would say to his weaker brothers and sisters, especially one of the latter whose throat seemed to be so constituted that she was obliged to cut up these boluses with a pair of scissors, 'Don't think, but gulp 'em down!'

So it was with everything else in life; Thomas did not think, he gulped it down. Thus in these matters of faith, if other young folk ventured to talk of 'allegory' or even to cast unhallowed doubts upon such points as those of the exact method of the appearance on this earth of their Mother Eve, or whether the sun actually did stand still at the bidding of Joshua, or the ark, filled with countless pairs of living creatures, floated to the top of Ararat, or Jonah, defying digestive juices, in fact abode three days in the interior of a whale, Thomas looked on them with a pitying smile and remarked that what had been written by Moses and other accepted prophets was enough for him.

Indeed a story was told of him when he was a boy at school which well exemplified this attitude. By way of lightening their labours a very noted geologist who had the art of interesting youthful audiences and making the rocks of the earth tell their own secular story, was brought to lecture to his House. This eminent man lectured extremely well. He showed how beyond a doubt the globe we inhabit, one speck of matter, floating in the sea of space, had existed for millions upon millions of years, and how by the evolutionary changes of countless ages it had at length become fitted to be the habitation of men, who probably themselves had lived and moved and had their being there for at least a million of years, perhaps much longer.

At the conclusion of the entrancing story the boys were invited to ask questions. Thomas Bull, a large, beetle-browed youth, rose at once and inquired of their titled and aged visitor, a man of world-wide reputation, why he thought it funny to tell them fairy tales. The old gentleman, greatly interested, put on his spectacles, and while the rest of the school gasped and the head master and other pedagogues stared amazed, studied this strange lad, then said:

'I am outspoken myself, and I like those who speak out when they do so from conviction; but, my young friend, why do you consider that I—well, exaggerate?'

'Because the Bible says so,' replied Thomas unabashed. 'The Bible tells us that the world was made in six days, not in millions of years, and that the sun and the moon and the stars were put in the sky to light it; also that man was created four thousand years B.C. Therefore, either you are wrong, sir, or the Bible is, and *I* prefer the Bible.'

The eminent scientist took off his spectacles and carefully put them away, remarking:

'Most logical and conclusive. Pray, young gentleman, do not allow any humble deductions of my own or others to interfere with your convictions. Only I believe it was Archbishop Ussher, not the Bible, who said that the world began about 4,000 B.C. I think that one day you may become a great man—in your own way. Meanwhile I might suggest that a certain sugaring of manners sweetens controversy.'

After this no more questions were asked, and the meeting broke up in confusion.

From all of which it will be gathered that since none of us is perfect, even in Thomas there were weak points. For instance, he had what is known as a 'temper', also he was blessed with a good idea of himself and his own abilities, and had a share of that intolerance by which this is so often accompanied.

In due course Thomas Bull became a theological student. Rarely was there such a student. He turned neither to left nor right, worked eight hours a day when he did not work ten, and took the highest possible degrees on every subject. Then he was ordained. About this time he chanced to hear a series of sermons by a colonial bishop that directed his mind towards the mission-field. This was after he had served as a deacon in an East End parish and become acquainted with savagery in its western form.

He consulted with his friends and his superiors as to whether his true call were not to the far parts of the earth. Unanimously they answered that they thought so; so unanimously that a mild fellow-labourer whom he bullied was stung to the uncharitable remark that almost it looked as though they wanted to be rid of him. Perhaps they did; perhaps they held that for energy so gigantic there was no fitting outlet in this narrow land.

But as it chanced there was another to be consulted, for by this time the Rev. Thomas Bull had become engaged to the only daughter of a deceased London trader—in fact, he had been a shop-keeper upon a large scale. This worthy citizen had re-married late in life, choosing, or being chosen by a handsome and rather fashionable lady of a somewhat higher class than his own, who was herself a widow. By her he had no issue, his daughter, Dorcas, being the child of his first marriage. Mr Humphreys, for that was his name, made a somewhat peculiar will, leaving all his fortune, which was considerable, to his young widow, charged, however, with an annuity of 300 pounds settled on his daughter Dorcas.

On the day before his death, however, he added a codicil which angered Mrs. Humphreys very much when she saw it, to the effect that if she re-married, three-fourths of the fortune were to pass to Dorcas at once, and that she or her heirs were ultimately to receive it all upon the decease of his wife.

The result of these testamentary dispositions was that one house, although it chanced to be large, proved too small to hold Mrs. Humphreys and her stepdaughter, Dorcas. The latter was a mild and timid little creature with a turned-up nose, light-coloured fluffy hair and an indeterminate mouth. Still there was a degree of annoyance and fashionable scorn at which her spirit rose. The end of it was that she went to live on her three hundred a year and to practise good works in the East End, being laudably determined to make a career for herself, which she was not in the least fitted to do.

Thus it was that Dorcas came into contact with the Rev. Thomas Bull. From the first time she saw her future husband he dominated and fascinated her. He was in the pulpit and really looked very handsome there with his burly form, his large black eyes and his determined, clean-shaven face. Moreover, he preached well in his own vigorous fashion.

On this occasion he was engaged in denouncing the vices and pettiness of modern woman—upper-class modern woman—of whom he knew nothing at all, a topic that appealed to an East End congregation. He showed how worthless was this luxurious stamp of females, what a deal they thought of dress and of other more evil delights. He compared them to the Florentines whom Savonarola (in his heart Thomas saw resemblances between himself and that great if narrow man) scourged till they wept in repentance and piled up their jewels and fripperies to be burned.

What do they do with their lives, he asked. Is there one in ten thousand of them who would abandon her luxuries and go forth to spread the light in the dark places of earth, or would even pinch herself to support others who did? And so on for thirty minutes.

Dorcas, listening and, reflecting on her stepmother, thought how marvellously true it all was. Had he known her personally, which so far as she was aware was not the case, the preacher could not have described her better. Also it was certain that Mrs. Humphreys and her friends had not the slightest intention of spreading any kind of light, unless it were that of their own eyes and jewels, or of going anywhere to do so, except perhaps to Monte Carlo in the spring.

How noble too was the picture he painted of the life of self-sacrifice and high endeavour that lay open to her sex. She would like to lead that higher life, being in truth a good-hearted little thing full of righteous impulses; only unfortunately she did not know how, for her present mild and tentative efforts had been somewhat disappointing in their fruits.

Then an inspiration seized her; she would consult Mr Bull.

She did so, with results that might have been anticipated. Within three months she and her mentor were engaged and within six married.

It was during those fervid weeks of engagement that the pair agreed, not without a little hesitation upon the part of Dorcas, that in due course he would become a missionary and set forth to convert the heathen in what he called 'Blackest Africa'. First, however, there was much to be done; he must go through a long course of training; he must acquaint himself with various savage languages, such as Swahili and Zulu, and so must she.

Oh! how poor Dorcas, who was not very clever and had no gift of tongues came to loathe those barbaric dialects. Still she worked away at them like a heroine, confining herself ultimately, with a wise and practical prescience, to learning words and sentences that dealt with domestic affairs, as as 'Light the fire.' 'Put the kettle on to boil.' 'Sister, have you chopped the wood?' 'Cease making so much noise in the kitchen-hut.' 'Wake me if you hear the lion eating our cow.' And so forth.

For more than a year after their marriage these preliminaries continued while Thomas worked like a horse, though it is true that Dorcas slackened her attention to Swahili and Zulu grammar in the pressure of more immediate affairs. Especially was this so after the baby was born, a girl, flaxen-haired like her mother, whom Thomas christened by the name of Tabitha, and who in after years became the 'Little Flower' of this history. Then as the time of departure drew near another thing happened. Her stepmother, Mrs. Humphreys, insisted upon going to a ball in Lent, where she caught a chill that developed into inflammation of the lungs and killed her.

The result of this visitation of Providence, as Thomas called it, was that Dorcas suddenly found herself a rich woman with an income of quite 2000 pounds a year, for her father had been wealthier than she knew. Now temptation took hold of her. Why, she asked herself, should Thomas depart to Africa to teach black people, when with his gifts and her means he could stop at home comfortably and before very long become a bishop, or at the least a dean?

Greatly daring, she propounded this matter to her husband, only to find that she might better have tried to knock down a stone wall with her head than induce him to change his plans. He listened to her patiently—unless over-irritated, a perfectly exasperating patience was one of his gifts—then said in a cold voice that he was astonished at her.

'When you were poor,' he went on, 'you vowed yourself to this service, and now because we are rich you wish to turn traitor and become a seeker after the fleshpots of Egypt. Never let me hear you mention the matter again.'

'But there is the baby,' she exclaimed. 'Africa is hot and might not agree with her.'

'Heaven will look after the baby,' he answered.

'That's just what I am afraid of,' wailed Dorcas.

Then they had their first quarrel, in the course of which, be it admitted, she said one or two spiteful things. For instance, she suggested that the real reason he wished to go abroad was because he was so unpopular with his brother clergymen at home, and especially with his superiors, to whom he was fond of administering lectures and reproofs.

It ended, of course, in her being crushed as flat as is a broken-winged butterfly that comes in the path of a garden roller. He stood up and towered over her.

'Dorcas,' he said, 'do what you will. Stay here if you wish, and enjoy your money and your luxuries. I sail on the first of next month for Africa. Because you are weak, do I cease to be strong?'

'I think not,' she replied, sobbing, and gave in.

So they sailed, first class—this was a concession, for he had intended to go third—but without a nurse; on that point he stood firm.

'You must learn to look after your own children,' he said, a remark at which she made a little face that meant more than he knew.

II

The career of Mr and Mrs. Bull during the next eight years calls for but little comment. Partly because Tabitha was delicate at first and must be within reach of doctors, they lived for the most part at various coast cities in Africa, where Thomas worked with his usual fervour and earnestness, acquiring languages which he learned to speak with considerable perfection, though Dorcas never did, and acquainting himself thoroughly with the local conditions in so far as they affected missionary enterprise.

He took no interest in anything else, not even in the history of the natives, or their peculiar forms of culture, since for the most part they have a secret culture of their own. All that was done with, he said, a turned page of the black and barbarous past; it was his business to write new things upon a new sheet. Perhaps it was for this reason that Thomas Bull never really came to understand or enter into the heart of a Zulu, or a

Basuto, or a Swahili, or indeed of any dark-skinned man, woman or child. To him they were but brands to be snatched from the burning, desperate and disagreeable sinners who must be saved, and he set to work to save them with fearful vigour.

His wife, although her vocabulary was still extremely limited and much eked out with English or Dutch words, got on much better with them.

'You know, Thomas,' she would say, 'they have all sorts of fine ideas which we don't understand, and are not so bad in their way, only you must find out what their way is.'

'I have found out,' he said grimly; 'it is a very evil way, the way of destruction. I wish you would not make such a friend of that sly black nurse-girl who tells me a lie once out of every three times she opens her mouth.'

For the rest Dorcas was fairly comfortable, as with their means she was always able to have a nice house in whatever town they might be stationed, where she could give tennis parties and even little lunches and dinners, that is if her husband chanced to be away, as often he was visiting up-country districts, or taking the duty there for another missionary who was sick or on leave. Indeed, in these conditions she came to like Africa fairly well, for she was a chilly little thing who loved its ample, all-pervading sunshine, and made a good many friends, especially among young men, to whom her helplessness and rather forlorn little face appealed.

The women, too, liked her, for she was kindly and always ready to help in case of poverty or other distresses. Luckily, in a way, she was her own mistress, since her fortune came to her unfettered by any marriage settlements; moreover, it was in the hands of trustees, so that the principal could not be alienated. Therefore she had her own account and her own cheque-book and used her spare money as she liked. More than one poor missionary's wife knew this and called her blessed, as through her bounty they once again looked upon the shores of England or were able to send a sick child home for treatment. But of these good deeds Dorcas never talked, least of all to her husband. If he suspected them, after one encounter upon some such matter, in which she developed a hidden strength and purpose, he had the sense to remain silent.

So things went on for years, not unhappily on the whole, for as they rolled by the child Tabitha grew acclimatised and much stronger. By this time, although Dorcas loved her husband as all wives should, obeying him in all, or at any rate in most things, she had come to recognise that he and she were very differently constituted. Of course, she knew that he was infinitely her superior, and indeed that of most people. Like everybody else she admired his uprightness, his fixity of purpose and his devouring energy and believed him to be destined to great things. Still, to tell the truth, which she often confessed with penitence upon her knees, on the whole she felt happier, or at any rate more comfortable, during his occasional absences to which allusion has been made, when she could have her friends to tea and indulge in human gossip without being called 'worldly.'

It only remains to add that her little girl Tabitha, a name she shortened into Tabbie, was her constant joy, especially as she had no other children. Tabbie was a bright, fair-haired little thing, clever, too, with resource and a will of her own, an improved edition of herself, but in every way utterly unlike her father, a fact that secretly annoyed him. Everybody loved Tabitha, and Tabitha loved everybody, not excepting the natives, who adored her. Between the Kaffirs and Tabitha there was some strong natural bond of sympathy. They understood one another.

At length came the blow.

It happened thus. Not far from the borders of Zululand but

in the country that is vaguely known as Portuguese Territory, was a certain tribe of mixed Zulu and Basuto blood who were called the Ama-Sisa, that is, the People of the Sisa. Now 'Sisa' in the Zulu tongue has a peculiar meaning which may be translated as 'Sent Away'. It is said that they acquired this name because the Zulu kings when they exercised dominion over all that district were in the habit of despatching large herds of the royal cattle to be looked after by these people, or in their own idiom to be *sisa'd*, i.e. agisted, as we say in English of stock that are entrusted to another to graze at a distance from the owner's home.

Some, however, gave another reason. In the territory of this tribe was a certain spot of which we shall hear more later, where these same Zulu kings were in the habit of causing offenders against their law or customs to be executed. Such also, like the cattle, were 'sent away,' and from one of these two causes, whichever it may have been, or perhaps from both, the tribe originally derived its name.

It was not a large tribe, perhaps there were three hundred and fifty heads of families in it, or say something under two thousand souls in all, descendants, probably, of a mild, peace-loving, industrious Basuto stock on to which had been grafted a certain number of the dominant, warlike Zulus who perhaps had killed out the men and possessed themselves of the Basuto women and their cattle. The result was that among this small people there were two strains, one of the bellicose type, who practically remained Zulus, and the other of the milder and more progressive Basuto stamp, who were in the majority.

Among these Sisas missionaries had been at work for a number of years, with results that on the whole were satisfactory. More than half of them had been baptised and were Christians of a sort; a church had been built; a more or less modern system of agriculture had been introduced, and most of the population wore trousers or skirts, according to sex. Recently, however, trouble had arisen over the old question of polygamy. The missionaries would not tolerate more than one wife, while the Zulu section of the tribe insisted upon the old prerogative of plural marriage.

The dispute had ended in something like actual fighting, in the course of which the church and the school were burnt, also the missionary's house. Because of these troubles this excellent man was forced to camp out in the wet, for it was the rainy season, and catching a chill, died suddenly of heart-failure following rheumatic fever just after he had moved into his new habitation, which consisted of some rather glorified native huts.

Subsequently to these events there came a petition from the chief of the tribe, a man called Kosa, whose name probably derived from the Zulu word Koos, which means chief or captain, addressed to the Church authorities and asking that a new Teacher might be sent to take the place of him who had died, also to rebuild the church and the school. If this were not done, said the messengers, the tribe would relapse into heathenism, since the Zulu and anti-Christian party headed by an old witch-doctor, named Menzi, was strong and gaining ground.

This was an appeal that could not be neglected, since hitherto the Sisa had been a spot of light in a dark place, as most of the surrounding peoples, who were of the old Zulu stock, remained heathen. If that light went out the chances were that they would continue to be so, whereas if it went on burning another result might be hoped, since from a spark a great fire may come. Therefore earnest search was made for a suitable person to deal with so difficult and delicate a situation, with the result that the lot fell upon the Rev. Thomas Bull.

Once his name was mentioned, it was acclaimed by all. He was the very man, they said, bold, determined, filled with a Jesuit's fiery zeal (although it need scarcely be explained that he hated Jesuits as a cat does mustard), one whom no witch-doctors would daunt, one, moreover, who being blessed with this world's goods would ask no pay, but on the contrary would perhaps contribute a handsome sum towards the re-building of the church. This, it may be explained, as the Mission itself scarcely possessed a spare penny with which to bless itself, was a point that could not be overlooked.

So Thomas was sent for and offered the post, after its difficulties and drawbacks had been fairly but diplomatically explained to him. He did not hesitate a minute, or at any rate five minutes; he took it at once, feeling that his call had come; also that it was the very thing for which he had been seeking. Up in that secluded spot in Portuguese Territory he would, he reflected, be entirely on his own, a sort of little bishop with no one to interfere with him, and able to have his own way about everything, which in more civilised regions he found he could not do. Here a set of older gentlemen, who were always appealing to their experience of natives, continually put a spoke into his wheel, bringing his boldest plans to naught. There it would be different. He would fashion his own wheel and grind the witch-doctor with his following to dust beneath its iron rim. He said that he would go at once, and what is more, he promised a donation of 1,000 pounds towards the rebuilding of the church and other burnt-out edifices.

'That is very generous of Bull,' remarked the Dean when he had left the room.

'Yes,' said another dignitary, 'only I think that the undertaking must be looked upon as conditional. I understand, well, that the money belongs to Mrs. Bull.'

'Probably she will endorse the bond as she is a liberal little woman,' said the Dean, 'and in any case our brother Bull, if I may be pardoned a vulgarism, will knock the stuffing out of that pestilent Menzi and his crowd.'

'Do you think so?' asked the other. 'I am not so certain. I have met old Menzi, and he is a tough nut to crack. He may 'knock the stuffing' out of him. Bull, sound as he is, and splendid as he is in many ways, does not, it seems to me, quite understand natives, or that it is easier to lead them than to drive them.'

'Perhaps not,' said the Dean, 'but in the case of these Sisas it is rather a matter of Hobson's choice, isn't it?'

So this affair was settled, and in due course Thomas received his letter of appointment as priest-in-charge of the Sisa station.

On his arrival home a few days later, where he was not expected till the following week, Thomas was so pre-occupied that he scarcely seemed to notice his wife's affectionate greeting; even the fact that both she and Tabitha were arrayed in smart and unmissionary-like garments escaped him. Dorcas also looked pre-occupied, the truth being that she had asked a few young people, officers and maidens of the place (alas! as it chanced, among them were no clergy or their wives and daughters), to play tennis that afternoon and some of them to stop to supper. Now she was wondering how her austere spouse would take the news. He might be cross and lecture her; when he was both cross and lectured the combination was not agreeable.

A few formal enquiries as to health and a certain sick person were made and answered. Dorcas assured him that they were both quite well, Tabitha especially, and that she had visited the afflicted woman as directed.

'And how was she, dear?' he asked.

'I don't know, dear,' she answered. 'You see, when I got to the house I met Mrs. Tomley, the Rector's wife, at the door, and she said, rather pointedly I thought, that she and her husband were looking after the case, and though grateful for the kind assistance you had rendered, felt that they need not trouble us any more, as the patient was a parishioner of theirs.'

'Did they?' said Thomas with a frown. 'Considering all

things—well, let it be.'

Dorcas was quite content to do so, for she was aware that her husband's good-heartedness was apt to be interpreted as poaching by some who should have known better, and that in fact the ground was dangerous.

'I have something to tell you,' she began nervously, 'about an arrangement I have made for this afternoon.'

Mr Bull, who was drinking a tumbler of water—he was a teetotaller and non-smoker, and one of his grievances was that his wife found it desirable to take a little wine for the Pauline reason—set it down and said:

'Never mind your afternoon arrangements, my dear; they are generally of a sort that can be altered, for *I* have something to tell *you*, something very important. My call has come.'

'Your call, dear. What call? I did not know that you expected anyone—and, by the way—'

She got no further, for her husband interrupted.

'Do not be ridiculous, Dorcas. I said call—not caller, and I use the word in its higher sense.'

'Oh! I understand, forgive me for being so stupid. Have they made you a bishop?'

'A bishop—'

'I mean a dean, or an archdeacon, or something!' she went on confusedly.

'No, Dorcas, they have not. I could scarcely expect promotion as yet, though it is true that I thought—but never mind, others no doubt have better claims and longer service. I have, however, been honoured with a most responsible duty.'

'Indeed, dear. What duty?'

'I have been nominated priest-in-charge of the Sisa Station.'

'O-oh! and where is that? Is it anywhere near Durban, or perhaps Maritzburg?'

'I don't exactly know at present, though I understand that

it is about six days' trek from Eshowe in Zululand, but over the border in Portuguese territory. Indeed, I am not sure that one can trek all the way, at least when the rivers are in flood. Then it is necessary to cross one of them in a basket slung upon a rope, or if the river is not too full, in a punt. At this season the basket is most used.'

'Great Heavens, Thomas! do you propose to put me and Tabbie in a basket, like St. Paul, and did you remember that we have just taken on this house for another year?'

'Of course I do. The families of missionaries must expect to face hardships, from which it is true circumstances have relieved you up to the present. It is therefore only right that they should begin now, when Tabitha has become as strong as any child of her age that I know. As for the house, I had forgotten all about it. It must be relet, or failing that we must bear the loss, which fortunately we can well afford.'

Dorcas looked at him and said nothing because words failed her, so he went on hurriedly.

'By the way, love, I have taken a slight liberty with your name. It appears that the church at Sisa, which I understand was quite a nice one built with subscriptions obtained in England by one of my predecessors who chanced to have influence or connections at home, has been recently burnt down together with the mission-house. Now the house can wait, since, of course, we can make shift for a year or two in some native huts, but obviously we must have a church, and as the Society is overdrawn it cannot help in the matter. Under these circumstances I ventured to promise a gift of 1,000 pounds, which it is estimated will cover the re-erection of both church and house.'

He paused awaiting a reply, but as Dorcas still said nothing, continued.

'You will remember that you told me quite recently that

you found you had 1,500 pounds to your credit, therefore I felt quite sure that you would not grudge 1,000 pounds of it to enable me to fulfil this duty—this semi-divine duty.'

'Oh!' said Dorcas. 'As a matter of fact I intended to spend that 1,000 pounds, or much of it, otherwise. There are some people here whom I wanted to help, but fortunately I had not mentioned this to them, so they will have to do without the money and their holiday; also the children cannot be sent to school. And, by the way, how is Tabbie to be educated in this far-away place?'

'I am sorry, dear, but after all private luxuries, including that of benevolence, must give way to sacred needs, so I will write to the Dean that the money will be forthcoming when it is needed. As for Tabitha's education, of course we will undertake it between us, at any rate for the next few years.'

'Yes, Thomas, since you have passed your word, or rather my word, the money will be forthcoming. But meanwhile, if you can spare me the odd 500 pounds, I suggest that I should stay here with Tabbie, who could continue to attend the college as a day-scholar, while you get us some place ready to live in among these savages, the Sneezers, or whatever they are called.'

'My dear,' answered Thomas, 'consider what you ask. You are in perfect health and so is our child. Would it not, then, be a downright scandal that you should stop here in luxury while your husband went out to confront grave difficulties among the Sisas—not the Sneezers—for I may tell you at once that the difficulties are very grave? There is a noted witch-doctor amongst this people named Menzi, who, I understand, is suspected of having burned down the mission-house, and probably the church also, because he said that it was ridiculous that an unmarried man like the late priest should have so large a dwelling to live alone. This, of course, was but a cunning excuse for his savage malevolence, but if another apparent celibate arrives, he might repeat the argument and its application. Also often these barbarians consider that a man who is not married *must* be insane! Therefore it is absolutely necessary that you and the child should be present with me from the first.'

'Oh! is it?' said Dorcas, turning very pink. 'Well, I am sorry to say that just now it is absolutely necessary that I should be absent from you, since I have a tennis party this afternoon—the officers of the garrison are coming and about half a dozen girls—and I must go to arrange about the tea.'

'A tennis party! A tennis party to those godless officers and probably equally godless girls,' exclaimed her husband. 'I am ashamed of you, Dorcas, you should be occupied with higher things.'

Then at last the worm turned.

'Do you know, Thomas,' she answered, springing up, 'that I am inclined to be ashamed of you too, who I think should be occupied in keeping your temper. You have accepted some strange mission without consulting me, you have promised 1,000 pounds of my money without consulting me, and now you scold me because I have a few young people to play tennis and stop to supper. It is unchristian, it is uncharitable, it is—too bad!' and sitting down again she burst into tears.

The Rev. Thomas who by now was in a really regal rage, not knowing what to say or do, glared about him. By ill-luck his eye fell upon a box of cigarettes that stood upon the mantelpiece.

'What are those things doing here?' he asked. 'I do not smoke, so they cannot be for me. Is our money—I beg your pardon—your money which is so much needed in other directions to be wasted in providing such unnecessaries—for officers and—idle girls? Oh—bless it all,' and seizing the offending cigarettes he hurled them through the open window, a scattered shower of white tubes which some Kaffirs outside instantly proceeded to collect.

Then he rushed from the house, and Dorcas went to get ready for her party. But first she sent a servant to buy another box of cigarettes. It was her first act of rebellion against the iron rule of the Rev. Thomas Bull.

### III

In the end, as may be guessed, Dorcas, who was a good and faithful little soul, accompanied her husband to the Sisa country. Tabitha went also, rejoicing, having learned that in this happy land there was no school. Dorcas found the journey awful, but really, had she but known it, it was most fortunate, indeed ideal. Her husband, who was a little anxious on the point, had made the best arrangements that were possible on such an expedition.

The wagon in which they trekked was good and comfortable, and although it was still the rainy season, fortune favoured them in the matter of weather, so that when they came to the formidable river, they were actually able to trek across it with the help of some oxen borrowed from a missionary in that neighbourhood, without having recourse to the dreaded rope-slung basket, or even to the punt.

Beyond the river they were met by some Christian Kaffirs of the Sisa tribe, who were sent by the Chief Kosa to guide them through the hundred miles or so of difficult country which still lay between them and their goal. These men were pleasant-spoken but rather depressed folk, clad in much-worn European clothes that somehow became them very ill. They gave a melancholy account of the spiritual condition of the Sisas, who since the death of their last pastor, they said, were relapsing rapidly into heathenism under the pernicious influence of Menzi, the witch-doctor. Therefore Kosa sent his greetings and prayed the new Teacher to hurry to their aid and put a stop to this state of things.

'Fear nothing,' said Thomas in a loud voice, speaking in Zulu, which by now he knew very well. 'I *will* put a stop to it.'

Then they asked him his name. He replied that it was Thomas Bull, which after the native fashion, having found out what bull meant in English, they translated into a long appellation which, strictly rendered, meant *Roaring-Leader-of-the-holy-Herd*. When he found this out, Thomas flatly declined any such unchristian title, with the result that, anxious to oblige, they christened him 'Tombool', and as 'Tombool' thenceforward he was known. (Dorcas objected to this name, but Tabitha remarked sagely that at any rate it was better than 'Tomfool'.)

This was to his face, but behind his back they called him *Inkunzi*, which means bull, and in order to keep up the idea, designated poor Dorcas *Isidanda*, that being interpreted signified a gentle-natured cow. To Tabitha they gave a prettier name, calling her *Imba* or Little Flower.

At first Dorcas was quite pleased with her title, which sounded nice, but when she came to learn what it meant it was otherwise.

'How can you expect me, Thomas, to live among a people who call me "a mild cow"?' she asked indignantly.

'Never mind, my dear,' he answered. 'In their symbolical way they are only signifying that you will feed them with the milk of human kindness,' a reply which did not soothe her at all. In fact, of the three the child alone was pleased, because she said that 'Opening Flower' was a prettier name than Tabbie, which reminded her of cats.

Thenceforward, following a track, for it could not be called a road, they advanced slowly, first over a mountain pass on the farther side of which the wagon nearly upset, and then across a great bush-clad plain where there was much game and the lions roared round them at night, necessitating great fires to frighten them away. These lions terrified Dorcas, a town-bred woman who had never seen one of them except in the Zoo, so much that she could scarcely sleep, but oddly enough Tabitha was not disturbed by them.

'God will not let us be eaten by a lion, will He, Father?' she asked in her simple faith.

'Certainly not,' he answered, 'and if the brute tries to do so I shall shoot it.'

'I'd rather trust to God, Father, because you know you can never hit anything,' replied Tabitha.

Fortunately, however, it never became necessary for Thomas to show his skill as a marksman, for when they got through the bushveld there were no more lions.

On the fourth day after they left the river they found themselves upon gentle sloping veld that by degrees led them upwards to high land where it was cold and healthy and there were no mosquitoes. For two days they trekked over these high lands, which seemed to be quite uninhabited save by herds of feeding buck, till at length they attained their crest, and below them saw a beautiful mimosa-clad plain which the guides told them was the Sisa Country.

'The Promised Land at last! It makes me feel like another Moses,' said Thomas, waving his arm.

'Oh, isn't it lovely!' exclaimed Tabitha.

'Yes, dear,' answered her mother, 'but—but I don't see any town.'

This indeed was the case because there was none, the Sisa kraal, for it could not be dignified by any other name, being round a projecting ridge and out of sight. For the rest the prospect was very fair, being park-like in character, with dotted clumps of trees among which ran, or rather wound, a silver stream that seemed to issue from between two rocky koppies in the distance.

These koppies, the guides told them, were the gates of Sisa Town. They neglected to add that it lay in a hot and unhealthy hill-ringed hollow beyond them, the site having originally been chosen because it was difficult to attack, being only approachable through certain passes. Therefore it was a very suitable place in which to kraal the cattle of the Zulu kings in times of danger. That day they travelled down the declivity into the plain, where they camped. By the following afternoon they came to the koppies through which the river ran, and asked its name. The answer was *Ukufa*.

'*Ukufa?*' said Thomas. 'Why, that means Death.'

'Yes,' was the reply, 'because in the old days this river was the River of Death where evil-doers were sent to be slain.'

'How horrible!' said Dorcas, for unfortunately she had overheard and understood this conversation.

By the side of the river was a kind of shelf of rock that was used as a road, and over this they bumped in their wagon, till presently they were past the koppies and could see their future home beyond. It was a plain some miles across, and entirely surrounded by precipitous hills, the river entering it through a gorge to the north. In the centre of this plain was another large koppie of which the river *Ukufa*, or Death, washed one side. Around this koppie, amid a certain area of cultivated land, stood the 'town' of the Christian branch of the Sisa. It consisted of groups of huts, ten or a dozen groups in all, set on low ground near the river, which suggested that the population might number anything between seven hundred and a thousand souls.

At the time that our party first saw it the sun was sinking, and had disappeared behind the western portion of the barricade of hills. Therefore the valley, if it may be so called, was plunged in a gloom that seemed almost unnatural when compared with the brilliant sky above, across which the radiant lights of an African sunset already sped like arrows, or rather like red and ominous spears of flame.

'What a dreadful place!' exclaimed Dorcas. 'Is our home to be here?'

'I suppose so,' answered Thomas, who to tell the truth for once was himself somewhat dismayed. 'It does look a little gloomy, but after all it is very sheltered, and home is what one makes it,' he added sententiously.

Here the conversation was interrupted by the arrival of the Chief and some of the Christian portion of the Sisa tribe, who having been warned of its approach by messenger, to the number of a hundred and fifty or so had advanced to meet the party.

They were a motley crowd clad in every kind of garment, ranging from a moth-eaten General's tunic to practically nothing at all. Indeed, one tall, thin fellow sported only a battered helmet of rusty steel that had drifted here from some European army, a *moocha* or waistbelt of catskins, and a pair of decayed tennis-shoes through which his toes appeared. With them came what were evidently the remains of the church choir, when there was a church, for they wore dirty fragments of surplices and sang what seemed to be a hymn tune to the strains of a decadent accordion.

The tune was long and ended in a kind of howl like to that of a disappointed jackal. When at length it was finished the Chief Kosa appeared. He was a middle-aged man, become prematurely old because he had lived too fast in his pre-Christian days, or so report said. Now he had a somewhat imbecile appearance, for his fingers twitched and when he spoke his mouth jerked up at the corners; also he kept looking over his shoulder as though he were afraid of something behind him.

Altogether he inspired Thomas with no confidence. Whatever else he might be, clearly he was not a staff for a crusader to lean upon.

Still he came forward and made a very nice speech, as a high-bred native noble, such as he was, can almost invariably do. With many pious expressions he welcomed the new Teacher, saying that he and his people, that is those of them who were Christians, would do their best to make him happy.

Thomas thanked him in appropriate language, adding that he on his part would do his best to promote their welfare and to save their souls.

Kosa replied that he was glad to hear it, because these needed saving, since most of the Sisa people were now servants of the devil. Since the last *Umfundisi*, or Teacher died, they had been walking the road to hell at a very great pace, marrying many wives, drinking gin and practising all kinds of witchcraft under the guidance of the *Isanusi* or doctor, Menzi. This man, he added, had burned down the church and the mission-house by his magic, though these had seemed to be destroyed by lightning.

With a proud gesture Thomas announced that he would soon settle Menzi and all his works, and that meanwhile, as the darkness was coming on, he would be glad if Kosa would lead them to the place where they were to sleep.

So they started, the accordion-man, playing execrably, leading the way, and trekked for about a mile and a half till they came to the koppie in the centre of the plain, reaching it by following the left bank of the river that washed its western face.

Passing between a number of tumbled walls built of loose stones, that once in bygone generations had sheltered the cattle of Chaka and other Zulu kings, they reached a bay in the side of the koppie that may have covered four acres of ground. Here by the edge of the river, but standing a little above it, were the burnt-out ruins of a building that by its shape had evidently been a church, and near to it other ruins of a school and of a house which once was the mission-station.

As they approached they heard swelling from within those cracked and melancholy walls the sound of a fierce, defiant chant which Thomas guessed must be some ancient Zulu war-song, as indeed it was. It was a very impressive song, chanted by many people, which informed the listeners that those who sung it were the King's oxen, born to kill the King's enemies, and to be killed for the King, and so forth; a deep-noted, savage song that thrilled the blood, at the first sound of which the accordion gave a feeble wail and metaphorically expired.

'Isn't that beautiful music, Father. I never heard anything like that before,' exclaimed Tabitha.

Before Thomas could answer, out from the ruined doorway of the Church issued a band of men—there might have been a hundred of them—clad in all the magnificent panoply of old-time Zulu warriors, with tall plumes upon their heads, large shields upon their arms, kilts about their middles, and fringes of oxtails hanging from their knees and elbows. They formed into a double line and advanced, waving broad-bladed assegais. Then at a signal they halted by the wagon and uttered a deep-throated salute.

In front of their lines was a little withered old fellow who carried neither shield nor spear, but only a black rod to which was bound the tail of a *wildebeeste*. Except for his *moocha* he was almost naked, and into his grey hair was woven a polished ring of black gum, from which hung several little bladders. Upon his scraggy neck was a necklace of baboon's teeth and amulets, whilst above the *moocha* was twisted a snake that might have been either alive or stuffed.

His face, though aged and shrunken, was fine-featured and full of breeding, while his hands and feet were very small;

his eyes were brooding, the eyes of a mystic, but when his interest was excited their glance was as sharp as a bradawl. Just now it was fixed on Thomas, who felt as if it were piercing him through and through. The owner of the eyes, as Thomas guessed at once, was Menzi, a witch-doctor very famous in those parts.

'Why are these men armed with spears? It is against the law for Kaffirs to carry spears,' he said to the Chief.

'This is Portuguese Territory; there is no law in Portuguese Territory,' answered Kosa with a vacant stare.

'Then we might be all murdered here and no notice taken,' exclaimed Thomas.

'Yes, Teacher. Many people have been murdered here: my father was murdered, and I dare say I shall be.'

'Who by?'

Kosa made no answer, but his vacant eyes rested for a little while on Menzi.

'Good God! what a country,' said Thomas to himself, looking at Dorcas who was frightened. Then he turned to meet Menzi, who was advancing towards them.

Casting a glance of contempt at Kosa, of whom he took no further notice, Menzi saluted the new-comers by lifting his hand above his head. Then with the utmost politeness he drew a snuff-box fashioned from the tip of a buffalo-horn out of a slit in the lobe of his left ear, extracted the wooden stopper and offered Thomas some snuff.

'Thank you, but I do not take that nastiness,' said Thomas.

Menzi sighed as though in disappointment, and having helped himself to a little, re-stoppered the horn and thrust it back into the lobe of his ear. Next he said, speaking in a gentle and refined voice:

'Greeting, Teacher, who, the messengers tell us, are called Tombool in your own language and in ours *Inkunzi*. A good name, for in truth you look like a bull. I am glad to see that you are made much more robust than was the last Teacher, and therefore will live longer in this place than he did. Though as for the lady-teacher—' and he glanced at the delicate-looking Dorcas.

Thomas stared at this man, to whom already he had taken a strong dislike. Then moved thereto either by a very natural outburst of temper, or perchance by a flash of inspiration, he replied:

'Yes, I shall live longer than did my brother, who died here and has gone to Heaven, and longer I think than you will.'

This personal remark seemed to take Menzi aback; indeed for a moment he looked frightened. Recovering himself, however, he said:

'I perceive, Teacher Tombool, that like myself you are a witch-doctor and a prophet. At present I do not know which of us will live the longer, but I will consult my Spirits and tell you afterwards.'

'Pray do not trouble to do so on my account, for I do not believe in your Spirits.'

'Of course you do not, Teacher. No doctor believes in another doctor's Spirits, since each has his own, and there are more Spirits than there are doctors. Teacher Tombool, I greet you and tell you at once that we are at war over this matter of Spirits. This tribe, Teacher, is a cleft log, yes, it is split into two. The Chief there, Kosa, sits on one half of the log with his Christians; I sit on the other half with the rest, who are as our fathers were. So if you wish to fight I shall fight with such weapons as I have. No, do not look at the spears—not with spears. But, if you leave me and my following alone, we shall leave you alone. If you are wise I think that you will do well to walk your own road and suffer us to walk ours.'

'On the contrary,' answered Thomas, 'I intend that all the Sisa people shall walk one road, the road that leads to Heaven.'

'Is it so, Teacher?' Menzi replied with a mysterious smile.

Then he turned his head and looked at the darkling river that just here, where it ran beneath an overhanging ledge of the koppie, was very deep and still. Thomas felt that there was a world of meaning in his look, though what it might be he did not know. Suddenly he remembered that this river was named Death.

After Menzi had looked quite a long while, once more he saluted as though in farewell, searching the faces of the three white people, especially Tabitha's, with his dreamy eyes and, letting them fall, searching the ground also. Near to where he stood grew a number of veld flowers, such as appear in their glory after the rains in Africa. Among these was a rare and beautiful white lily. This lily Menzi plucked, and stepping forward, presented it to Tabitha, saying:

'A flower for the Flower! A gift to a child from one who is childless!'

Her father saw and meditated interference. But he was too late; Tabitha had already taken the lily and was thanking Menzi in his own tongue, which she knew well enough, having been brought up by Zulu nurses. He smiled at her, saying:

'All Spirits, black or white, love flowers.'

Then for a third time he saluted, not the others, but Tabitha, with more heartiness than before, and turning, departed, followed by his spearmen, who also saluted Tabitha as they filed in front of her.

It was a strange sight to see these great plumed men lifting their broad spears to the beautiful bright-haired child who stood there holding the tall white lily in her hand as though it were a sceptre.

## IV

When Menzi and his company had departed, vanishing round the corner of the koppie, Thomas again asked the Chief where they were to sleep, an urgent matter as darkness was now approaching.

Kosa answered with his usual vagueness that he supposed in the hut where the late Teacher had died after the mission-house was burnt down. So they trekked on a little way, passing beneath the shelf of rock that has been mentioned as projecting from that side of the koppie which overhung the stream, where there was just room for a wagon to travel between the cliff and the water.

'What a dark road,' said Dorcas, and one of the Christian natives who understood some English, having been the body-servant of the late missionary—it was he with the accordion—replied in Zulu:

'Yes, Lady; this rock is called the Rock of Evildoers, because once those accused of witchcraft and others were thrown from it by the order of the King, to be eaten by the crocodiles in that pool.' 'But,' he added, brightening up, 'do not be afraid, for there are no more Zulu kings and we have hunted away the crocodiles, though it is true that there are still plenty of wizards who ought to be thrown from the rock,' and he looked over his shoulder in the direction Menzi had taken, adding in a low voice, 'You have just seen the greatest of them, Lady.'

'How horrible!' said Dorcas for the second time.

A few yards farther on they emerged from this tunnel-like roadway and found themselves travelling along the northern face of the koppie. Here, surrounded by a fence, stood the Chief's kraal, and just outside of it a large, thatched hut with one or two smaller huts at its back. It was a good hut of its sort, being built after the Basuto fashion with a projecting roof and a doorway, and having a kind of verandah floored with beaten lime.

'This was the Teacher's house,' said Kosa as the wagon halted.

'I should like to look inside it at once,' remarked Dorcas doubtfully, adding, 'Why, what's that?' and she pointed to a suspicious-looking, oblong mound that was covered with weeds, over which she had almost stumbled.

'That is the grave of the late Teacher, Lady. We buried him here because Menzi's people took up the bones of those who were in the churchyard and threw them into the river,' explained Kosa.

Dorcas looked as though she were going to faint, but Thomas, rising to the occasion, remarked:

'Come on, dear. The dead are always with us, and what better company could we have than the dust of our sainted predecessor.'

'I would rather have his room,' murmured Dorcas, and gathering herself together, proceeded to the hut.

Somebody opened the door with difficulty, and as it seemed to be very dark within, Thomas struck a match, by the light of which Dorcas peered into the interior. Next second she fell back into his arms with a little scream.

'Take me away!' she said. 'The place is full of rats.'

He stared; it was quite true. There, sitting up upon the dead missionary's bed, was a singularly large rat that did not seem in the least frightened by their appearance, whilst other creatures of the same tribe scuttled about the floor and up the walls.

Dorcas slept, or did not sleep, that night in the wagon with Tabitha, while Thomas took his rest beneath it as well as a drizzling rain that was falling would allow.

Such was the beginning of the life of the Bull family in

Sisa-Land, not an encouraging beginning, it will be admitted, though no worse and perhaps much better than that which many missionaries and their families are called upon to face in various regions of the earth. What horror is there that missionaries have not been called upon to endure? St. Paul tells us of his trials, but they are paralleled, if not surpassed, even in the present day.

Missionaries, however good, may not always be wise folk; the reader might even think the Rev. Thomas Bull to be no perfect embodiment of wisdom, sympathy or perhaps manners, but taking them as a class they are certainly heroic folks, who endure many things for small reward, as we reckon reward. In nothing perhaps do they show their heroism and faith more greatly than in their persistent habit of conveying women and young children into the most impossible places of the earth, there to suffer many things, not exclusive, occasionally, of martyrdom. At least the Protestant section of their calling does this; the Roman Catholics are wiser. In renouncing marriage these save themselves from many agonies, and having only their own lives and health at stake, are perhaps better fitted to face rough work in rough places.

Even Thomas Bull, not a particularly sensitive person, was tempted more than once to arrive at similar conclusions during his period of service in Sisa-land, although neither he nor his wife or child was called upon to face the awful extremities that have confronted others of his cloth; for instance, another Thomas, one Owen, who was a missionary in Zululand at the time when Dingaan, the King, massacred Retief and his Boers beneath his eyes.

On the following morning Thomas crept out from beneath his wagon, not refreshed, it is true, but filled with a renewed and even more fiery zeal. During those damp hours of unrest he had reflected much and brought the whole position into perspective, a clear if a narrow perspective. The Chief with whom he had to deal evidently was a fool, if not an imbecile, and the Christians who remained after a generation of teaching were for the most part poor creatures, the weak-kneed amongst this mixed-blood tribe, probably those of the milder Basuto origin.

Such strength as remained in the people, who were, after all, but a dwindling handful marooned in a distant spot, was to be found among those of the old Zulu stock. They were descendants of the men sent by the Kings Chaka and Dingaan to keep an eye upon the humble Basuto slaves, whose duty it was to herd the royal cattle, the men, too, to whom was entrusted the proud but hateful business of carrying out the execution of persons that, for one reason or another, it was not desirable to kill at home.

The individuals detailed for these duties were for the most part of high blood, inconvenient persons, perhaps, whom it was desired to move to a distance. Thus, as Thomas Bull soon learned, Menzi was said to be no less a man than the grandson of the King Dingaan himself, one whose father had developed troublesome ambitions, but whose life had been spared because his mother was a favourite with the King.

Hence some of the grandson's pride, which was enhanced by the fact that in his youth he had been trained in medicine and magic by a certain Zikali, alias 'Opener-of-Roads', who was said to have been the greatest witch-doctor that ever lived in Zululand, and through him had acquired, or perhaps developed inherent psychic gifts, that were in any case considerable.

In the end, however, he had returned to his petty tribe, neglecting larger opportunities, as Thomas learned, because of some woman to whom he was attached at home. It seemed, however, that he might as well have stayed away, since on his arrival he found that this woman had become one of the

Chief's wives, for which reason he afterwards killed that Chief, Kosa's father, and possessed himself of the woman, who died immediately afterwards, as Menzi suspected by poisoning. It was principally for this reason that he hated Kosa, his enemy's son, and all who clung to him; and partly because of that hatred and the fear that it engendered Kosa and his people had turned Christian, hoping to protect themselves thus against Menzi and his wizardries. Also for this dead woman's sake, Menzi had never married again.

Thomas did not learn all these details, and others that need not be mentioned, at once, but by the time he crept out from under that wagon he had guessed enough to show that he was face to face with a very tough proposition, and being the man he was, he girded his loins to meet it, vowing that he would conquer Menzi or die in the attempt.

That very morning he called a council of the Christians and set to work with a will. The first thing to do was to make the late missionary's huts habitable, which did not take long, and the next to commence the rebuilding of the church. Thomas, true to his principles, insisted on beginning with the church and letting the mission-house stand over, although Dorcas, small blame to her, complained at being obliged to live for an indefinite time in a hut like a Kaffir woman. However, as usual, she was obliged to give way.

As it chanced, here there was little difficulty about building operations, for stone and wood and *tambuki* grass for thatching were all at hand in plenty. Also the Basuto section of the Sisa, as is common among that race, were clever masons and carpenters, some of them having followed those trades in Natal and the more settled places in Zululand, where dwellings had to be erected. Moreover, they possessed wagons, and now that the dry season was approaching were able to fetch stores of every kind from the borders of Natal. Lastly, thanks to Dorcas's banking account, money was by comparison no object, an unusual circumstance where missionaries are concerned.

So all the week Thomas laboured at these matters and at making himself acquainted with his congregation, and all Sunday he held open-air services or taught in the ruins of the old church.

Thus in the midst of so many new interests matters went on not uncomfortably, and Dorcas became more or less reconciled to her life. Still she could never get over her loathing of the place which she believed to be ill-omened, perhaps because of its gloomy aspect, coupled with the name of the river and the uses to which it had been put, after all not so very long ago. Naturally, also, this distaste was accentuated by the unlucky circumstances of their arrival.

Tabitha, too, was really happy, since she loved this wild free life, and having been brought up amongst Kaffirs and talking their language almost as well as she did her own, soon she made many friends.

Perhaps it was a sense that the information would not be well received by her father that prevented her from mentioning that the greatest of those friends was the old witch-doctor, Menzi, whom she often met when she was rambling about the place. Or it may have been pure accident, since Thomas was too busy to bother about such trifles, while her mother, who of course knew, kept her own counsel. The truth is that though he was a heathen witch-doctor, Dorcas liked old Menzi better than any other native in the district, because she said, quite truly, that he was a gentleman, however sinful and hard-hearted he might be. Moreover, with a woman's perception she felt that if only he were a friend, at a pinch he might be worth all the others put together, while if he were an enemy, conversely the same applied.

So it came about that in the end there arose a very strange

state of affairs. Menzi hated Thomas and did all he could to thwart him. He liked Dorcas and did all he could to help her, while the child Tabitha he came to worship, for some reason he never revealed, which was hidden in the depths of his secret soul; indeed ere long had she been his own daughter he could not have loved her more. It was he who amongst many other things gave her the pretty carved walking-stick of black and white *umzimbeet* wood, also the two young blue cranes and the kid that afterwards were such pets of hers, and with them the beautiful white feathers of a cock ostrich that had been killed on the veld. In the same way it was he who sent milk and eggs to Dorcas when she was at her wits' end for both, which more than once were found mysteriously at the door of their hut, and not any of his Christian flock, as Thomas fondly imagined.

Thus things went on for a while.

Meanwhile Thomas found this same Menzi a stumbling-block and a rock of offence. Whenever he tried to convert man, woman, or child he was confronted with Menzi or the shadow of Menzi. Thus those with whom he was arguing would ask him why he could not work miracles like Menzi. Let him show them pictures in the fire, or tell them who had stolen their goods or where they would find their strayed cattle, and perhaps they would believe him. And so forth.

At length Thomas grew exasperated and announced publicly that he credited nothing of this magic, and that Menzi was only a common cheat who threw dust into their eyes. If Menzi could perform marvels, let him show these marvels to him, Thomas, and to his wife, that they might judge of them for themselves.

Apparently this challenge was repeated to the witch-doctor. At least one morning a few days later, when Thomas went out accompanied by Dorcas and Tabitha, to meet the Chief Kosa and others and to discuss with them whether ultimately the mission-house should be rebuilt upon the old site or elsewhere, he found a great concourse of people, all or nearly all the tribe indeed, assembled on a level place where in the old days stood one of the great kraals designed to hold the king's cattle. Out of the crowd emerged Kosa, looking rather sillier than usual, and of him Thomas inquired why it was gathered. Was it to consult with him about the mission-house?

'No, Teacher,' answered the Chief, 'Menzi has heard that you call him a cheat, and has come to show that he is none, assembling all the people that they may judge between you and him.'

'I do not want to see his tricks,' said Thomas angrily. 'Tell him to go away.'

'Oh, Teacher!' replied Kosa, 'that would not be wise, for then everyone would believe that Menzi's magic is so great that you are afraid even to look upon it. It is better to let him try. Perhaps if you pray hard he will fail, for his spirits will not always come when he calls them.'

Thomas hesitated, then, being bold by nature, determined that he would see the thing through. After all, Menzi was an impostor and nothing else, and could work no more magic than he could himself. Here was a providential opportunity to expose him. So followed by the others he advanced into the crowd, which made way for him.

In an open space in its centre, sat Menzi wearing all his witch-doctor's trappings, bladders in his hair, snakeskins tied about him, and the rest, but even in this grotesque attire still managing to look dignified. With him were several acolytes or attendants, one of them an old woman, also peculiarly arrayed and carrying hide bags that contained their master's medicines. He rose as they came, saluted Thomas and smiled at Dorcas and Tabitha, very sweetly at the latter.

'O Teacher,' he said, 'my ears hear that you say that I am

a liar and a cheat who have no wonders at my command; to whom the Spirits never speak and who deceives the people. Now, Teacher, I have come here that it may be seen whether you are right or I am right. If your magic is greater than mine, then I can do nothing and I will eat the dust before you. But if mine prevails, then perhaps all these will say that you are the cheat, not I. Also it is true that I am not a great magician as was my master, Zikali, the Opener-of-Roads, and cannot show you things worthy to be seen. Nor will I smell out evil-doers, witches and wizards, since then the people might kill them, and I think that there are some here who deserve to die in the ancient fashion. No, I will not do this, since it is not right that those with you,' here he glanced at Dorcas and Tabitha, 'should look upon the sight of blood, even in this land where the White-man's law has no power. Still there are little things that may serve to amuse you for an hour and hurt no one. Have any of you lost anything, for instance?'

'Yes, I have,' said Tabitha with a laugh.

'Is it so, Little Flower? Then be silent and do not say what you have loSt Have you told any what you have lost?'

'No,' answered Tabitha, 'because I was afraid I should be scolded.'

'There, *Imba*, there, Little Flower, even that is too much, because you see the old cheat might guess something from your words. Yes, he might guess that it is something of value that you have lost, such as a bracelet of gold, or the thing that ticks, on which you white people read the time. Nay, be silent and do not let your face move lest I should read it. Now let us see what it is that you have lost.'

Then he turned to his confederates, as Thomas called them, and began to ask them questions which need not be set out in detail. Was it an animal that the Little Flower had lost? No, it was not an animal, the Spirits told him that it was not. Was it an article of dress? No, they did not think it was an article of dress, yet the Spirits seemed to suggest that it had something to do with dress. Was it a shoe? Was it scissors? Was it a comb? Was it a needle? No, but it was something that had to do with needles. What had to do with needles? Thread. Was it thread? No, but something that had to do with thread. Was it a silver shield which pushed the needle that drew the thread?

Here Tabitha could contain herself no longer, but clapped her hands and cried out delightedly:

'Yes, that's it. It's my thimble.'

'Oh! very well,' said Menzi, 'but it is easy to discover what is lost and hard to find it.'

Then followed another long examination of the assessors or acolytes, or witch-doctor's chorus, by which it was established at length that the thimble had been lost three days before, when Tabitha was sitting on a stone sewing, that she believed it had fallen into a crevice of rocks, and so forth.

After this the chorus was silent and Menzi himself took up the game, apparently asking questions of the sky and putting his ear to the ground for an answer.

At length he announced: (1) That the thimble was not among the rocks; (2) That it was not lost at all.

'But it is, it is, you silly old man,' cried Tabitha excitedly. 'I have hunted everywhere, and I cried about it because I haven't got another, and can't buy one here, and the needle hurts my finger.'

Menzi contemplated her gravely as though he were looking her through and through.

'It is *not* lost, Little Flower. I see it; you have it now. Put your hand into the pocket of your dress. What do you find there?'

'Nothing,' said Tabitha. 'That is, nothing except a hole.'

'Feel at the bottom of your dress, there on the right. No, a little more to the front. What do you feel there?'

'Something hard,' said Tabitha.

'Take this knife and cut the lining of your dress where you feel the hard thing. Ah! there is the silver shield which you have been carrying about with you all these days.'

The crowd murmured approval. Dorcas exclaimed: 'Well, I never!' and Thomas looked first puzzled, then angry, then suspicious.

'Does the Teacher think that the Floweret and the old doctor have made a plot together?' asked Menzi. 'Can a sweet Flower make plots and tell lies like the old doctor? Well, well, it is nothing. Now let us try something better. My bags, my bags.'

Thomas made as though he would go away, but Menzi stopped him, saying:

'No, doubters must stay to see the end of their doubts. What shall I do? Ah! I have it.'

Then from one of the bags he drew out a number of crooked black sticks that looked like bent ebony rulers, and built them up criss-cross in a little pile upon the ground. Next he found some bundles of fine dried grass, which he thrust into the interstices between the sticks, as he did so bidding one of his servants to run to the nearest hut and bring a coal of fire upon a sherd.

'A match will not do,' he said. 'White men have touched it.'

Presently the burning ember arrived, and muttering something, Menzi blew upon it as though to keep it alight.

'Now, White Teacher,' he said in a voice that had suddenly become commanding, 'think of something. Think of what you will, and I will show it to you.'

'Indeed,' said Thomas with a smile. 'I have thought of something; now make good your words.'

Menzi thrust the ember into the haylike fibres and blew. They caught and blazed up fiercely, making an extraordinarily large flame considering the small amount of the kindling. The ebony-like sticks also began to blaze. Menzi grew excited.

'My Spirit, come to me; my Spirit, come to me!' he cried. 'O my Spirit, show this White Teacher Tombool that I am not a cheat!'

He ran round and round the fire; he leapt into the air, then suddenly shouted: 'My Spirit has entered into me; my Snake is in my breast!'

All his excitement went; he grew quite calm, almost cataleptic. Holding his thin hands over the fire, slowly he let them fall, and as he did so the fierce flames died down.

'It's going out,' said Tabitha.

Menzi smiled at her and lifted his hands again. Lo! the fire that seemed to be dead leapt up after them in a fierce blaze. Again he dropped his hands and the fire died away. Then he moved his arms to and fro and it came back, following the motions of his arms as though he drew it by a string.

'Have you thought, White Teacher? Have you thought?' he asked. 'Good! Arise, smoke!'

Behold, instead of the clear flame appeared a fan-shaped column of dense white smoke, behind which Menzi vanished, all except his outstretched hands.

'Look on to the smoke, White people, and do you, Little Flower, tell me what you see there,' he called from behind this vaporous veil.

Tabitha stared, they all stared. Then she cried out:

'I see a room, I see an old man in a clergyman's coat reading a letter. Why, it is the Dean whom we used to know in Natal. There's the wart on his nose and the tuft of hair that hangs down over his eye, and he's reading a letter written by Father. I know the writing. It begins, "My dear Dean, Providence has appointed me to a strange place"—'

'Is that what you see also, Teacher?' asked Menzi. 'And if so, is it what you pictured in your thought?'

Thomas turned away and uttered something like a groan, for indeed he had thought of the Dean and of the letter he had written to him a month before.

'The Teacher is not satisfied,' said Menzi. 'If he had seen all he thought of, being so good and honest, he would tell us. There is some mistake. My Spirit must have deceived me. Think of something else, Teacher, and tell the lady, and the child Imba, and Kosa, and another, what it is you are thinking of. Go aside and tell them where I cannot hear.'

Thomas did so—in some way he felt compelled to do so.

'I am going to think of the church as I propose it shall be when finished according to the plans I have made,' he said hoarsely. 'I am going to think of it with a belfry spire roofed with red tiles and a clock in the tower, and I am going to think of the clock as pointing to the exact hour of noon. Do you all understand? It is impossible that this man should know of how I mean to build that spire and about the clock, because until this moment no one knew except myself. If he can show me that, I shall begin to believe that he is inspired by his master, the devil. Do you all understand?'

They said they did, and Menzi called out:

'Be quick, White Teacher. Be quick, I grow tired. My Spirit grows tired. The smoke grows tired. Come, come, come!'

They returned and stood in front of the fire, and in obedience to Menzi's motions once more the fan of smoke arose. On it grew something nebulous, something uncertain that by degrees took the form of a church. It was not very clear, perhaps because Thomas found it difficult to conceive the exact shape of the church as it would be when it was finished, or only conceived it bit by bit. One thing, however, was very distinct in his mind, and that was the proposed spire and the clock. As a result, there was the spire standing at the end of the shadowy church vivid and distinct. And there was the clock with its two copper hands exactly on the stroke of noon!

'Tell me what you see, Little Flower,' said Menzi in a hollow voice.

'I see what Father told me he would think of, a church and the spire of the church, and the clock pointing to twelve.'

'Do you all see that,' asked Menzi, 'and is it what the Teacher said he would think about?'

'Yes, Doctor,' they answered.

'Then look once more, for *I* will think of something. I will think of that church falling. Look once more.'

They looked, and behold the shadowy fabric began to totter, then it seemed to collapse, and last of all down went the spire and vanished in the smoke.

'Have you seen anything, O people?' said Menzi, 'for standing behind this smoke I can see nothing. Mark that it is thick, since through it I am invisible to you.'

This was true, since they could only perceive the tips of his outstretched fingers appearing upon each side of the smoke-fan.

'Yes,' they answered, 'we have seen a church fall down and vanish.'

'That was my thought,' said Menzi; 'have I not told you that was the thought my Spirit gave me?'

'This is black magic, and you are a fiend!' shouted Thomas, and was silent.

'Not so, Tombool, though it is true that I have gifts which you clever White people do not understand,' answered Menzi.

By degrees the smoke melted away, and there on the ground were the ten or twelve crooked pieces of ebony that they had seen consumed, now to all appearance quite untouched by the flame. There too on their farther side lay Menzi, shining with perspiration, and in a swoon or sleeping.

'Come away,' said Thomas shortly, and they turned to go, but at this moment something happened.

Menzi, it will be remembered, had given Tabitha a kid of a long-haired variety of goat peculiar to these parts. This little creature had already grown attached to its mistress and walked about after her, in the way which pet goats have. It had followed her that morning, but not being interested in tricks or magic, engaged itself in devouring herbs that grew amongst the tumbled stones of the old kraal.

Suddenly Menzi recovered from his faint or seizure and, looking up, directed his attendants to return the magical ebony rods which burned without being consumed to one of the hide bags that contained his medicines. The assembly began to break up amidst a babel of excited talk.

Tabitha looked round for her goat, and perceiving it at a little distance, ran to fetch it, since the creature, being engaged in eating something to its taste, would not come at her call. She seized it by the neck to drag it away, with the result that its fore-feet, obstinately set upon the wall, overturned a large stone, revealing a great puff adder that was sleeping there.

The reptile thus disturbed instantly struck backwards after the fashion of its species, so that its fangs, just missing Tabitha's hands, sank deep into the kid's neck. She screamed and there was a great disturbance. A native ran forward and pinned down the puff-adder with his walking-stick of which the top was forked. The kid immediately fell on to its side, and lay there bleeding and bleating. Tabitha began to weep, calling out, 'My goat is killed,' between her sobs.

Menzi, distinguishing her voice amid the tumult, asked what was the matter. Someone told him, whereon he commanded that the kid should be brought to him and the snake also. This was done, Tabitha following her dying pet with her mother, for by now Thomas had departed, taking no heed of these events, which perhaps he was too disturbed to notice.

'Save my goat! Save my goat, O Menzi!' implored Tabitha.

The old witch-doctor looked at the animal, also at the hideous puff-adder that had been dragged along the ground in the fork of the stick.

'It will be hard, Little Flower,' he said, 'seeing that the goat is bitten in the neck and this snake is very poisonous. Still for your sake I will try, although I fear that it may prove but a waste of good medicine.'

Then he took one of his bags and from it selected a certain packet wrapped in a dried leaf, out of which he shook some grey powder. Seizing the kid, which seemed to be almost dead, he made an incision in its throat over the wound, and into it rubbed some of this powder. Next he spat upon more of the powder, thus turning it into a paste, and opening the kid's mouth, thrust it down its throat, at the same time muttering an invocation or spell.

'Now we must wait,' he said, letting the kid fall upon the ground, where it lay to all appearance dead.

'Is that powder any good?' asked Dorcas rather aimlessly.

'Yes, it is very good, Lady; a medicine of power of which I alone have the secret, a magic medicine. See, I will show you. Except the *immamba*, the ring-snake that puffs out its head, this one is the most deadly in our country. Yet I do not fear it. Look!'

Leaning forward, he seized the puff-adder, and drawing it from beneath the fork, suffered it to strike him upon the breast, after which he deliberately killed it with a stone. Then he took some of the grey powder and rubbed it into the punctures; also put more of it into his mouth, which he swallowed.

'Oh!' exclaimed Dorcas, 'he will die,' and some of the Christian Kaffirs echoed her remark.

But Menzi did not die at all. On the contrary, after shivering a few times he was quite himself, and, indeed, seemed rather brighter than before, like a jaded business man who has drunk a cocktail.

'No, Wife of Tombool,' he said, 'I shall not die; every year I doctor myself with this magic medicine that is called *Dawa*, after which all the snakes in Sisa-Land—remember that they are many, Little Flower—may bite me if they like.'

'Is it your magic or is it the medicine that protects you?' asked Dorcas.

'Both, Lady. The medicine *Dawa* is of no use without the magic words, and the magic words are of no use without the medicine. Therefore alone in all the land I can cure snake bites, who have both medicine and magic. Look at your goat, Little Flower. Look at your goat!'

Tabitha looked, as did everyone else. The kid was rising to its feet. It rose, it baa'd and presently began to frisk about its mistress, like Menzi apparently rather brighter than before.

V

A year had gone by, during which time, by the most heroic exertions, Thomas Bull had at length succeeded in rebuilding the church. There it stood, a very nice mission-church, constructed of sun-dried bricks neatly plastered over, cool and spacious within, for the thatched roof was lofty, beautifully furnished (the font and the pulpit had been imported from England), and finished off with the spire and clock of his dreams, the latter also imported from England and especially adjusted for a hot climate.

Moreover, there was a sweet and loud-throated bell upon which the clock struck, with space allowed for the addition of others that must wait till Thomas could make up his mind to approach Dorcas as to the provision of the necessary funds. Yes, the church was finished, and the Bishop of those parts had made a special journey to consecrate it at the hottest season of the year, and as a reward for his energy had contracted fever and nearly been washed away in a flooded river.

Only one thing was lacking, a sufficient congregation to fill this fine church, which secretly the Bishop, who was a sensible man, thought would have been of greater value had it been erected in any of several other localities that he could have suggested. For alas! the Christian community of Sisa-Land did not increase. Occasionally Thomas succeeded in converting one of Menzi's followers, and occasionally Menzi snatched a lamb from the flock of Thomas, with the result that the scales remained even neither going up nor down.

The truth was, of course, that the matter was chiefly one of race; those of the Sisas in whom the Basuto blood preponderated became Christian, while those who were of the stubborn Zulu stock, strengthened and inspired by their prophet Menzi, remained unblushingly heathen.

Still Thomas did not despair. One day, he told himself, there would be a great change, a veritable landslide, and he would see that church filled with every Zulu in the district. Needless to say, he wished him no ill, but Menzi was an old man, and before long it might please Providence to gather that accursed wizard to his fathers. For that he was a wizard of some sort Thomas no longer doubted, a person directly descended from the Witch of Endor, or from some others of her company who were mentioned in the Bible. There was ample authority for wizards, and if they existed then why should they they not continue to do so? Since he could not explain it, Thomas swallowed the magic, much as in his boyhood he used to swallow the pills.

Yes, if only Menzi were removed by the will of Heaven, which really, thought Thomas, must be outraged by such proceedings, his opportunity would come, and 'Menzi's herd,' as the heathens were called in Sisa-land, would be added to his own. The Bishop, it is true, was not equally sanguine, but said nothing to discourage zeal so laudable and so uncommon.

It was while his Lordship was recovering from the sharp bout of fever which he had developed in a new and mosquito-haunted hut with a damp floor that had been especially erected for his accommodation, that at last the question of the rebuilding of the mission-house came to a head, which it could not do while all the available local labour, to say nothing of some hired from afar, was employed upon the church.

Thomas, it was true, wished to postpone it further, pointing out that a school was most necessary, and that after all they had grown quite accustomed to the huts and were fairly comfortable in them.

On this point, however, Dorcas was firm; indeed, it would not be too much to say that, having already been disappointed once, she struck with all the vigour of a trade-unioniSt She explained that the situation of the huts on the brink of the river was low and most unhealthy, and that in them she was becoming a victim to recurrent attacks of fever. He, Thomas, might be fever-proof, as indeed she thought he was. It was true also that Tabitha had been extraordinarily well and grown much ever since she came to Sisa-Land, which puzzled her, inasmuch as the place was notoriously unhealthy for children, even if they were of native blood. Indeed, in her agitation she added an unwise remark to the effect that she could only explain their daughter's peculiar health by supposing that Menzi had laid a 'good charm' upon her, as all the natives believed, and he announced publicly that he had done.

This made Thomas very angry, admittedly not without cause. Forgetting his conversation to a belief in the reality of Menzi's magic, he talked in a loud voice about the disgrace of being infected with vile, heathen superstitions, such as he had never thought to hear uttered by his wife's Christian lips. Dorcas, however, stuck to her point, and enforced it by a domestic example, adding that the creatures which in polite society are called 'bed-pests,' that haunted the straw of the huts, tormented her while Tabitha never had so much as a single bite.

The end of it was that the matter of mission-house *versus* huts was referred to the Bishop for his opinion. As the teeth of his Lordship were chattering with ague resulting, he knew full well, from the fever he had contracted in the said huts, Dorcas found in him a most valuable ally. He agreed that a mission-house ought to be built before the school or anything else, and suggested that it should be placed in a higher and better situation, above the mists that rose from the river and the height to which mosquitoes fly.

Bowing to the judgment of his superior, which really he heard with gratitude, although in his zeal and unselfishness he would have postponed his own comfort and that of his family till other duties had been fulfilled, Thomas replied that he knew only one such place which would be near enough to the Chief's town. It was on the koppie itself, about fifty feet above the level of and overhanging the river, where he had noted there was always a breeze, even on the hottest day, since the conformation of this hill seemed to induce an unceasing draught of air. He added that if his Lordship were well enough, they might go to look at the site.

So they went, all of them. Ascending a sloping, ancient path that was never precipitous, they came to the place, a flat tableland that perhaps measured an acre and a half, which by some freak of nature had been scooped out of the side of the koppie, and was backed by a precipitous cliff in which were caves. The front part of this plateau, that which approached to and overhung the river, was of virgin rock, but the acre or so behind was filled with very rich soil that in the course of centuries had been washed down from the sides of the koppie, or resulted from the decomposition of its material.

'The very place,' said the Bishop. 'The access is easy. The

house would stand here—no need to dig deep foundations in this stone, and behind, when those trees have been cleared away, you could have a beautiful and fertile garden where anything will grow. Also, look, there is a stream of pure water running from some spring above. It is an ideal site for a house, not more than three minutes' walk from the church below, the best I should say in the whole valley. And then, consider the view.'

Everyone agreed, and they were leaving the place in high spirits, Dorcas, who had household matters to attend, having already departed, when whom should they encounter but Menzi seated on a stone just where the path began to descend. Thomas would have passed him without notice as one with whom he was not on speaking terms, but the Bishop, having been informed by Tabitha who he was, was moved by curiosity to stop and interchange some words with him, as knowing his tongue perfectly, he could do.

'Sakubona' (that is, 'good day'), he said politely.

Menzi rose and saluted with his habitual courtesy, first the Bishop, then the others, as usual reserving his sweetest smile for Tabitha.

'Great Priest,' he said at once, 'I understand that the Teacher Tombool intends to build his house upon this place.'

The Bishop wondered how on earth the man knew that, since the matter had only just been decided by people talking in English, but answered that perhaps he might do so.

'Great Priest,' went on Menzi in an earnest voice, 'I pray you to forbid the Teacher Tombool from doing anything of the sort.'

'Why, friend?' asked the Bishop.

'Because, Great Priest, this place is haunted by the spirits of the dead, and those who live here will be haunted also. Hearken. I myself when I was young have seen evil-doers brought from Zululand and hurled from that rock, blinded and broken-armed, by order of the King. I say that scores have been thrown thence to be devoured by the crocodiles in the pool below. Will such a sight as this be pleasant for white eyes to look upon, and will such cries as those of the evil-doers who have "gone down" be nice for white ears to hear in the silence of the night?'

'But, my good man,' said the Bishop, 'what you say is nonsense. These poor creatures are dead, "gone down" as you say, and do not return. We Christians have no belief in ghosts, or if they exist we are protected from them.'

'None at all,' interposed Thomas boldly and speaking in Zulu. 'This man, my Lord, is at his old tricks. For reasons of his own he is trying to frighten us; for my part I will not be frightened by a native witch-doctor and his rubbish, even if he does deal with Satan. With your permission I shall certainly build the mission-house here.'

'Quite right, of course, quite right,' said the Bishop, though within himself he reflected that evidently the associations of the spot were disagreeable, and that were he personally concerned, perhaps he should be inclined to consider an alternative site. However, it was a matter for Mr Bull to decide.

'I hear that Tombool will not be turned from his purpose. I hear that he will still build his house upon this rock. So be it. Let him do so and see. But this I say, that Imba, the Floweret, shall not be haunted by the *Isitunzi* (the ghosts of the dead) who wail in the night,' said Menzi.

He advanced to Tabitha, and holding his hands over her he cried out:

'Sweet eyes, be blind to the *Isitunzi*. Little ears, do not hear their groans. Spirits, build a garden fence about this flower and keep her safe from all night-prowling evil things. Imba, Little Flower, sleep softly while others lie awake and tremble.'

Then he turned and departed swiftly.

'Dear me!' said the Bishop. 'A strange man, a very strange

man. I don't know quite what to make of him.'

'I do,' answered Thomas, 'he is a black-hearted villain who is in league with the devil.'

'Yes, I dare say—I mean as to his being a villain, that is according to our standards—but does your daughter—a clever and most attractive little girl, by the way—think so? She seemed to look on him with affection—one learns to read children's eyes, you know. A very strange man, I repeat. If we could see all his heart we should know lots of things and understand more about these people than we do at present. Has it ever struck you, Mr Bull, how little we white people *do* understand of the black man's soul? Perhaps a child can see farther into it than we can. What is the saying—"a little child shall lead them", is it not? Perhaps we do not make enough allowances. "Faith, Hope and Charity, these three, but the greatest of these is charity"— or love, which is the same thing. However, of course you are quite right not to have been frightened by his silly talk about the *Isitunzi*, it would never do to show fear or hesitation. Still, I am glad that Mrs. Bull did not hear it; you may have noticed that she had gone on ahead, and if I were you I should not repeat it to her, since ladies are so nervous. Tabitha, my dear, don't tell your mother anything of all this.'

'No, Bishop,' answered Tabitha, 'I never tell her all the queer things that Menzi says to me when I meet him, or at least not many of them.'

'I wish I had asked him if he had a cure for your local fever,' said the Bishop with a laugh, 'for against it, although I have taken so much that my ears buzz, quinine cannot prevail.'

'He has given me one in a gourd, Bishop,' replied Tabitha confidentially, 'but I have never taken any, because you see I have had no fever, and I haven't told mother, for if I did she would tell father' (Thomas had stridden ahead, and was out of hearing), 'and he might be angry because he doesn't like Menzi, though I do. Will you have some, Bishop? It is well corked up with clay, and Menzi said it would keep for years.'

'Well, my dear,' answered the Bishop, 'I don't quite know. There may be all sorts of queer things in Mr Menzi's medicine. Still, he told you to drink it if necessary, and I am absolutely certain that he does not wish to poison *you*. So perhaps I might have a try, for really I feel uncommonly ill.'

So later on, with much secrecy, the gourd was produced, and the Bishop had 'a try.' By some strange coincidence he felt so much better after it that he begged for the rest of the stuff to comfort him on his homeward journey, which ultimately he accomplished in the best of health.

That most admirable and wide-minded prelate departed, and so far as history records was no more seen in Sisa-Land. But Thomas remained, and set about the building of the house with his usual vigour. Upon the Death Rock, as it was called, in course of time he erected an excellent and most serviceable dwelling, not too large but large enough, having every comfort and convenience that his local experience could suggest and money could supply, since in this matter the cheque-book of the suffering Dorcas was entirely at his service.

At length the house was finished, and with much rejoicing the Bull family, deserting their squalid huts, moved into it at the commencement of the hot season. After the first agitations of the change and of the arrangement of the furniture newly-arrived by wagon, they settled down very comfortably, directing all their energies towards the development of the garden, which had already been brought into some rough order during the building of the house.

One difficulty, however, arose at once. For some mysterious reason they found that not a single native servant would sleep in the place, no, not even Tabitha's personal attendant, who adored her. Every soul of them suddenly developed a sick mother or other relative who would instantly expire if deprived of the comfort of their society after dark. Or else they themselves became ailing at that hour, saying they could not sleep upon a cliff like a rock-rabbit.

At any rate, for one cause or another off they went the very moment that the sun vanished behind the western hills, nor did they re-appear until it was well up above those that faced towards the east.

At least this happened for one night. On the following day, however, a pleasant-looking woman named Ivana, whom they knew to be of good repute, though of doubtful religion, as sometimes she came to church and sometimes she did not, appeared and offered her services as 'night-dog'—that is what she called it—to Tabitha, saying that she did not mind sleeping on a height. Since it was inconvenient to have no one about the place from dark to dawn, and Dorcas did not approve of Tabitha being left to sleep alone, the woman, whose character was guaranteed by the Chief Kosa and the elders of the church, was taken on at an indefinite wage. To the matter of pecuniary reward, indeed, she seemed to be entirely indifferent.

For the rest she rolled herself in blankets, native fashion, and slept across Tabitha's door, keeping so good a watch that once when her father wished to enter the room to fetch something after the child was sleep, she would not allow even him to do so. When he tried to force a way past her, suddenly Ivana became so threatening that he thought she was about to spring at him. After this he wanted to dismiss her, but Dorcas said it only showed that she was faithful, and that she had better be left where she was, especially as there was no one to take her place.

So things went on till the day of full moon. On that night Ivana appeared to be much agitated, and insisted that Tabitha should go to bed earlier than was usual. Also after she was asleep Dorcas noticed that Ivana walked continually to and fro in front of the door of the child's room and up and down the veranda on to which its windows opened, droning some strange song and waving a wand.

However, at the appointed hour, having said their prayers, Dorcas and her husband went to bed.

'I wonder if there is anything strange about this place,' remarked Dorcas. 'It is so very odd that no native will stop here at night except that half-wild Ivana.'

'Oh! I don't know,' replied Thomas with a yawn, real or feigned. 'These people get all sorts of ideas into their silly heads. Do stop twisting about and go to sleep.'

At last Dorcas did go to sleep, only to wake up again suddenly and with great completeness just as the church clock below struck three, the sound of which she supposed must have roused her. The brilliant moonlight flooded the room, and as for some reason she felt creepy and disturbed, Dorcas tried to occupy her mind by reflecting how comfortable it looked with its new, imported furnishings, very different from that horrible hut in which they had lived so long.

Then her thoughts drifted to more general matters. She was heartily tired of Sisa-Land, and wished earnestly that her husband could get a change of station, which the Bishop had hinted to her would not be impossible—somewhere nearer to civilisation. Alas! he was so obstinate that she feared nothing would move him, at any rate until he had converted 'Menzi's herd,' who were also obstinate, and remained as heathen as ever. Indeed why, with their ample means, should they be condemned to perpetual exile in these barbarous places? Was there not plenty of work to be done at home, where they might make friends and live decently?

Putting herself and her own wishes aside, this existence was not fair to Tabitha, who, as she saw, watching her with a mother's eye, was becoming impregnated with the native atmosphere. She who ought to be at a Christian school now talked more Zulu than she did English, and was beginning to look at things from the Zulu point of view and to use their idioms and metaphors even when speaking her own tongue. She had become a kind of little chieftainess among these folk, also, Christian and heathen alike. Indeed, now most of them spoke of her as the Maiden *Inkosikazi*, or Chieftainess, and accepted her slightest wish or order as law, which was by no means the case where Dorcas herself and even Thomas were concerned.

In fact, once or twice they had been driven to make a request through the child, notably upon an important occasion that had to do with the transport-riding of their furniture, to avoid its being left for a couple of months on the farther side of a flooded river. The details do not matter, but what happened was that when Tabitha intervened that which had been declared to be impossible proved possible, and the furniture arrived with wonderful celerity. Moreover, Tabitha made no request; as Dorcas knew, though she hid it from Thomas, she sent for the headmen, and when they were seated on the ground before her after their fashion, Menzi among them, issued an order, saying:

'What! Are my parents and I to live like dogs without a kennel or cattle that lack a winter kraal, because you are idle? Inspan the wagons and fetch the things or I shall be angry. *Hamba*—Go!'

Thereon they rose and went without argument, only lifting their right hands above their heads and murmuring, '*Ikosikaas! Umame!* (Chieftainess! Mother!) we hear you.' Yes, they called Tabitha 'Mother!'

It was all very wrong, thought Dorcas, but she supposed, being a pious little person, that she must bear her burden and trust to Providence to free her from it, and she closed her eyes to wipe away a tear.

When Dorcas opened them again something very strange seemed to have happened. She felt wide awake, and yet knew that she must be dreaming because the room had disappeared. There was nothing in sight except the bare rock upon which the house stood. For instance, she could see the gorge behind as it used to be before they made it into a garden, for she recognised some of the very trees that they had cut down. Moreover, from one of the caves at the end of it issued a procession, a horrible procession of fierce-looking, savage warriors, with spears and knobkerries, who between them half dragged, half carried a young woman and an elderly man.

They advanced. They passed within a few feet of her, and observing the condition of the woman and the man, she saw that these must be led because for a certain reason they could not see where to go,—oh! never mind what she saw.

The procession reached the edge of the rock where the railing was, only now the railing had gone like the house. Then for the first time Dorcas heard, for hitherto all had seemed to happen in silence.

'Die, *Umtakati!* Die, you wizard, as the King commands, and feed the river-dwellers,' said a deep voice.

There followed a struggle, a horrible twisting of shapes, and the elderly man vanished over the cliff, while a moment later from below came the noise of a great splash.

Next the girl was haled forward, and the words of doom were repeated. She seemed to break from her murderers and stagger to the edge of the precipice, crying out:

'O Father, I come!'

Then, with one blood-curdling shriek, she vanished also, and again there followed the sound of a great splash that slowly echoed itself to silence.

All had passed away, leaving Dorcas paralysed with terror, and wet with its dew, so that her night-gear clung to her body. The room was just as it had been, filled with the soft moonlight and looking very comfortable.

'Thomas!' gasped his wife, 'wake up.'

'I *am* awake,' he answered in his deep voice, which shook a little. 'I have had a bad dream.'

'What did you dream? Did you see two people thrown from the cliff?'

'Something of that sort.'

'Oh! Thomas, Thomas, I have been in hell. This place is haunted. Don't talk to me of dreams. Tabitha will have seen and heard too. She will be driven mad. Come to her.'

'I think not,' answered Thomas.

Still he came.

At the door of Tabitha's room they found the woman Ivana, wide-eyed, solemn, silent.

'Have you seen or heard anything, Ivana?' asked Thomas.

'Yes, Teacher,' she answered, 'I have seen what I expected to see and heard what I expected to hear on this night of full moon, but I am guarded and do not fear.'

'The child! The child!' said Dorcas.

'The *Inkosikazi* Imba sleeps. Disturb her not.'

Taking no heed, they thrust past her into the room. There on her little white bed lay Tabitha fast asleep, and looking like an angel in her sleep, for a sweet smile played about her mouth, and while they watched she laughed in her dreams. Then they looked at each other and went back to their own chamber to spend the rest of the night as may be imagined.

Next morning when they emerged, very shaken and upset, the first person they met was Ivana, who was waiting for them with their coffee.

'I have a message for you, Teacher and Lady. Never mind

who sends it, I have a message for you to which you will do well to give heed. Sleep no more in this house on the night of full moon, though all other nights will be good for you. Only the little Chieftainess Imba ought to sleep in this house on the night of full moon.'

So indeed it proved to be. No suburban villa could have been more commonplace and less disturbed than was their dwelling for twenty-seven nights of every month, but on the twenty-eighth they found a change of air desirable. Once it is true the stalwart Thomas, like Ajax, defied the lightning, or rather other things that come from above—or from below. But before morning he appeared at the hut beneath the koppie announcing that he had come to see how they were getting on, and shaking as though he had a bout of fever.

Dorcas asked him no questions (afterwards she gathered that he had been favoured with quite a new and very varied midnight programme); but Tabitha smiled in her slow way. For Tabitha knew all about this business as she knew everything that passed in Sisa-Land. Moreover, she laughed at them a little, and said that *she* was not afraid to sleep in the mission-house on the night of full moon.

What is more, she did so, which was naughty of her, for on one such occasion she slipped back to the house when her parents were asleep, followed only by her 'night-dog,' the watchful Ivana, and returned at dawn just as they had discovered that she was missing, singing and laughing and jumping from stone to stone with the agility of her own pet goat.

'I slept beautifully,' she cried, 'and dreamed I was in heaven all night.'

Thomas was furious and rated her till she wept. Then suddenly Ivana became furious too and rated him.

Should he be wrath with the Little Chieftainess Imba, she asked him, because the *Isitunzis*, the spirits of the dead, loved her as did everything else? Did they not understand that the Floweret was unlike them, one adored of dead and living, one to be cherished even in her dreams, one whom 'Heaven Above,' together with those who had 'gone below,' built round with a wall of spells?—and more of such talk, which Thomas thought so horrible and blasphemous that he fled before its torrent.

But when he came back calmer he said no more to Tabitha about her escapade.

It was a long while afterwards, at the beginning of the great drought, that another terrible thing happened. On a certain calm and beautiful day Tabitha, who still grew and flourished, had taken some of the Christian children to a spot on the farther side of the koppie, where stood an old fortification originally built for purposes of defence. Here, among the ancient walls, with the assistance of the natives, she had made a kind of summer-house as children love to do, and in this house, like some learned eastern pundit in a cell, a very pretty pundit crowned with a wreath of flowers, she sat upon the ground and instructed the infant mind of Sisa-Land.

She was supposed to be telling them Bible stories to prepare them for their Sunday School examination, which, indeed, she did with embellishments and in their own poetic and metaphorical fashion. The particular tale upon which she was engaged, by a strange coincidence, was that from the Acts which narrates how St. Paul was bitten by a viper upon the Island of Melita, and how he shook it off into the fire and took no hurt.

'He must have been like Menzi,' said Ivana, who was present, whereon Tabitha's other attendant, who was also with her as it was daytime, started an argument, for being a Christian she was no friend to Menzi, whom she called a 'dirty old witch-doctor.'

Tabitha, who was used to these disputations, listened smiling, and while she listened amused herself by trying to thrust a stone into a hole in the side of her summer-house, which was formed by one of the original walls of the old kraal.

Presently she uttered a scream, and snatched her arm out of the hole. To it, or rather to her hand, was hanging a great hooded snake of the cobra variety such as the Boers call *ringhals*. She shook it off, and the reptile, after sitting up, spitting, hissing and expanding its hood, glided back into the wall. Tabitha sat still, staring at her lacerated finger, which Ivana seized and sucked.

Then, bidding one of the oldest of the children to take her place and continue sucking, Ivana ran to a high rock a few yards away which overlooked Menzi's kraal, that lay upon a plain at a distance of about a quarter of a mile, and called out in the low, ringing voice that Kaffirs can command, which carries to an enormous distance.

'Awake, O Menzi! Come, O Doctor, and bring with you your *Dawa*. The little Chieftainess is bitten in the finger by a hooded snake. The Floweret withers! Imba dies!'

Almost instantly there was a disturbance in the kraal and Menzi appeared, following by a man carrying a bag. He cried back in the same strange voice:

'I hear. I come. Tie string or grass round the lady Imba's finger below the bite. Tie it hard till she screams with pain.'

Meanwhile the Christian nurse had rushed off over the crest of the koppie to fetch Thomas and Dorcas, or either of them. As it chanced she met them both walking to join Tabitha in her bower, and thus it came about that they reached the place at the same moment as did old Menzi bounding up the rocks like a *klipspringer* buck, or a mountain sheep. Hearing him, Thomas turned in the narrow gateway of the kraal and asked wildly:

'What has happened, Witch-doctor?'

'This has happened, White-man,' answered Menzi, 'the Floweret has been bitten by a hooded snake and is about to die.

Look at her,' and he pointed to Tabitha, who notwithstanding the venom sucking and the grass tied round her blackened finger, sat huddled-up, shivering and half comatose.

'Let me pass, White-man, that I may save her if I can,' he went on.

'Get back,' said Thomas, 'I will have none of your black magic practised on my daughter. If she is to live God will save her.'

'What medicines have you, White-man?' asked Menzi.

'None, at least not here. Faith is my medicine.'

Dorcas looked at Tabitha. She was turning blue and her teeth were chattering.

'Let the man do his best,' she said to Thomas. 'There is no other hope.'

'He shan't touch her,' replied her husband obstinately.

Then Dorcas fired up, meek-natured though she was and accustomed though she was to obey her husband's will.

'I say that he shall,' she cried. 'I know what he can do. Don't you remember the goat? I will not see my child die as a sacrifice to your pride.'

'I have made up my mind,' answered Thomas. 'If she dies it is so decreed, and the spells and filth of a heathen cannot save her.'

Dorcas tried to thrust him aside with her feeble strength, but big and burly, he stood in the path like a rock, blocking the way, with the stone entrance walls of the little pleasure-house on either side of him.

Suddenly the old Zulu, Menzi, became rather terrible; he drew himself up; he seemed to swell in size; his thin face grew set and fierce.

'Out of the path, White-man!' he said, 'or by Chaka's head I will kill you,' and from somewhere he produced a long, thin-bladed knife of native iron fixed on a buck's horn.

'Kill on, Wizard,' shouted Thomas. 'Kill if you can.'

'Listen,' said Dorcas. 'If our daughter dies because of you, then I have done with you. We part for ever. Do you understand?'

'Yes, I understand,' he answered heavily. 'So be it.'

Tabitha behind them made some convulsive noise. Thomas turned and looked at her; she was slowly sinking down upon her side. His face changed. All the rage and obstinacy went out of it.

'My child! Oh, my child!' he cried, 'I cannot bear this. Love is stronger than all. When I come up for judgment, may it be remembered that love is stronger than all!'

Then he stepped out of the gateway, and sat down upon a stone hiding his eyes with his hand.

Menzi threw down the knife and leapt in, followed by his servant who bore his medicines, and the woman Ivana. He did his office; he uttered his spells and invocations, he rubbed *Dawa* into the wound, and prising open the child's clenched teeth, thrust more of it, a great deal more, down her throat, while all three of them rubbed her cold limbs.

About half an hour afterwards he came out of the place followed by Ivana, who carried Tabitha in her strong arms; Tabitha was very weak, but smiling, and with the colour returning to her cheeks. Of Thomas he took no notice, but to Dorcas he said:

'Lady, I give you back your daughter. She is saved. Let her drink milk and sleep.'

Then Thomas, whose judgment and charity were shaken for a while, spoke, saying:

'As a man and a father I thank you, Witch-doctor, but know that as a priest I swear that I will never have more to do with you, who, I am sure, by your arts, can command these reptiles to work your will and have planned all this to shame me. No, not even if you lay dying would I come to visit you.'

Thus stormed Thomas in his wrath and humiliation, believing that he had been the victim of a plot and not knowing that he would live bitterly to regret his words.

'I see that you hate me, Teacher,' said Menzi, 'and though here I do not find the gentleness you preach, I do not wonder; it is quite natural. Were I you I should do the same. But you are Little Flower's father—strange that she should have grown from such a seed—and though we fight, for that reason I cannot hate you. Be not disturbed. Perhaps it was the sucking of the wound and the grass tied round her finger which saved her, not my spells and medicine. No, no, I cannot hate you, although we fight for mastery, and you pelt me with vile words, saying that I charmed a deadly *immamba* to bite Little Flower whom I love, that I might cure her and make a mock of you. Yet I do hate that snake which bit the maiden Imba of its own wickedness, the hooded *immamba* that you believe to be my familiar, and it shall die. Man,' here he turned to his servant, 'and you, Ivana and the others, pull down that wall.'

They leapt to do his bidding, and presently discovered the *ringhals* in its hole. Heedless of its fangs and writhings, Menzi sprang at it with a Zulu curse, and seizing it, proceeded to kill it in a very slow and cruel fashion.

## VI

The great drought fell upon Sisa-Land like a curse from Heaven. For month after month the sun beat fiercely, the sky was as brass, and no rain fell. Even the dews seemed to depart. The springs dried up. The river Ukufa, the river called Death, ceased to flow, so that water could only be found in its deepest hollows. The pool beneath the Rock of Evildoers, the Death Rock, sank till the bones of those who had been murdered there many years before appeared as the crocodiles had left them. Cattle died because there was no grass; cows ceased to give their milk even where they could be partially fed and watered, so that the little children died also. Even in the dampest situations the crops withered, till at last it became certain that unless rain fell within a month, before another cold season had gone by there would be starvation everywhere. For the drought was widespread, and therefore corn could not be sent from other districts, even if there were cattle to draw it.

Every day Thomas put up prayers for rain in the church, and on two occasions held special services for this purpose. These were better attended than any others had ever been, because his congregation felt that the matter was extremely urgent, affecting them all, and that now was the time when, whatever happened to the heathen, good Christians like themselves should be rewarded.

However this did not chance, since the drought went on as fiercely as before.

Menzi was, of course, a rain-doctor, a 'Heaven-herd' of the highest distinction; one who, it was reputed, could by his magic cause the most brazen sky to melt in tears. His services had been called in by neighbouring tribes, with the result, it was rumoured, that those tribes had been rewarded with partial showers. Also with great ceremony he had gone through his rites for the benefit of the heathen section of the Sisa people. Behold! by some curious accident on the following day a thunderstorm had come up, and with it a short deluge of rain which sufficed to make it certain that the crops in those fields on which it fell would keep alive, at any rate for a while.

But mark what happened. As is not uncommon in the case of thunder showers, this rain fell upon the lands which the heathen cultivated on one side of the koppie, whereas those that belonged to the Christian section upon the other side received not a single drop. The unjust were bedewed, the just were left dry as bones. All that they received was the lightning, which killed an old man, one of the best Christians in the place. The limits of the torrent might have been marked off with a line. When it had passed, to the heathen right stood pools of water; to the Christian left there was nothing but blowing dust.

Now these Christians, weak-kneed some of them, began to murmur, especially those who, having passed through a similar experience in their youth, remembered what starvation meant in that country. Religion, they reflected, was all very well, but without mealies they could not live, and without Kaffir corn there would be no beer. Indeed, metaphorically, before long they passed from murmurs to shouting, and their shouts said this: Menzi must be invited to celebrate a rain-service in his own fashion for the benefit of the entire tribe.

Thomas argued in vain. He grew angry; he called them names which doubtless they deserved; he said that they were spiritual outcasts. By this time, being frantic, his flock did not care what he said. Either Menzi must come, they explained, or they would turn heathen. The Great One in the sky could work as well through Menzi as through him, Tombool or anybody else. Menzi *must* come.

Thomas threatened to excommunicate them all, a menace which did not amount to much as they were already excommunicating themselves, and when they remained obstinate, told them that he would have nothing to do with this rain-making business, which was unholy and repugnant to him. He told them, moreover, that he was certain that their wickedness would bring some judgment upon them, in which he proved to be right.

The end of it was that Menzi was summoned, and arrived with a triumphant smile, saying that he was certain he could put everything in order, and that soon they would have plenty of rain, that is, if they all attended his invocations and made him presents suitable to so great an occasion.

The result was that they did attend them, man, woman and child, seated in a circle in that same old kraal where the witch-doctor had so marvellously shown pictures upon the smoke. Each of them also brought his gift in his hand, or, if it were a living thing, drove it before him.

Thomas went down and addressed them in the midst of a sullen silence, calling them wicked and repeating his belief that they would bring a judgment on their own heads, they who were worshipping Baal and making offerings to his priest.

After he had talked himself hoarse, Menzi said mildly that if the Teacher Tombool had finished he would get to business. Why should the Teacher be angry because he, Menzi, offered to do what the Teacher could not—save the land from starving? And as for the gifts to himself, did not White Teachers also receive pay and offerings at certain feasts?

Then, making a gesture of despair, Thomas returned to his house, and with Dorcas and Tabitha watched the savage ceremony from the edge of the cliff that overhung the river, or rather what had been the river. He could not see much of it because they were too far away, but he perceived those apostate Christians prostrating themselves at Menzi's order, probably, he reflected, to make prayers to the devil. In fact they were not doing this, but only repeating Menzi's magical chants with appropriate gestures, as for countless ages their forefathers had done upon similar occasions.

Next an unfortunate black goat was dragged forward by the horns, a very thin black goat, and its throat was cut over a little fire, a sacrifice that suggested necromancy of the most Satanic sort.

After this Thomas and his family went back into the house and shut the windows, that they might not hear the unholy shoutings of the misguided mob. When they went out again

Menzi had departed, and so had the others. The place was empty.

The following day was Sunday, and Thomas locked the church on the inner side, and read the service with Dorcas and Tabitha for sole congregation. It was a melancholy business, for some sense of evil seemed to hang over all three of them, also over everybody else, for the Christians went about with dejected looks and not one person spoke to them. Only Ivana came at night as usual to sleep with Tabitha, though even she said nothing.

Next morning they woke up to find the heavens black with clouds, heavy, ominous clouds; the truth being that the drought was drawing to its natural end. Thomas noted this, and reflected bitterly how hard it was that this end should not have come twenty-four hours earlier. But so events had been decreed and he was helpless.

By midday it began to rain, lightly at first, and from his rock he could see the people, looking unnatural and distorted in that strange gloom, for the clouds had descended almost to the earth, rushing about, holding out their hands as though to clasp the blessed moisture and talking excitedly one to the other. Soon they were driven into their huts, for the rain turned into a kind of waterspout. Never had such rain been known in Sisa-Land.

All that afternoon it poured, and all the night with ever-increasing violence; yes, and all the following morning, so that by noon Thomas's rain-gauge showed that over twelve inches had fallen in about twenty-four hours, and it was still raining. Water rushed down from the koppie; even their well-built house could not keep out the wet, and, to the despair of Dorcas, several of the rooms were flooded and some of the new furniture was spoiled. The river beneath had become a raging torrent, and was rising every hour. Already it was over its banks, and the water had got into the huts of the Chief's kraal and the village round it, so that their occupants were obliged to seek safety upon the lower rocks of the koppie, where they sat shivering in the wet.

Night came at last, and through the darkness they heard cries as of people in distress. The long hours wore away till dawn, a melancholy dawn, for still it rained, though more lightly now, and no sun could be seen.

'Father,' cried Tabitha, who, clad in oilskins, had gone a little way down the road, 'come here and look.'

He went. The child pointed to the village below, or rather what had been the village, for now there was none. It had gone and with it Kosa's kraal; the site was a pool, the huts had vanished, all of them, and some of the roofs lay upon the sides of the koppie, looking like overturned coracles. Only the church and the graveyard remained, for those stood on slightly higher ground by the banks of the river.

A little while later a miserable and dejected crowd arrived at the mission-house, wrapped up in blankets or anything else that they had managed to save.

'What do you want?' asked Thomas.

'Teacher,' replied the Chief Kosa, with twitching face and rolling eyes, 'we want you to come down to the church and pray for us. Our houses are gone, our fields are washed away. We want you to come to pray for us, for more rain is gathering on the hills and we are afraid.'

'You mean that you are cold and wish to take refuge in the church, of which I have the key. You have sought rain and now you have got rain, such rain as you deserve. Why do you complain? Go to your witch-doctor and ask him to save you.'

'Teacher, come down to the church and pray for us,' they wailed.

In the end Thomas went, for his heart was moved to pity,

and Dorcas and Tabitha went with him.

They entered the church, wading to it through several inches of water, and the service of intercession began, attended by every Christian in the place—except a few who were drowned—a miserable and heartily repentant crowd.

While it was still in progress suddenly there was a commotion, and Menzi himself rushed into the church. It was the first time he had ever entered there.

'Come forth!' he cried. 'Come forth if you would save your lives. The water has eaten away the ground underneath this Heaven-house. It falls! I say it falls!'

Then he peered about him in the shadowed place till he found Tabitha. Leaping at her, he threw his long thin arms round her and bore her from the church. The others began to follow swiftly, and as Menzi passed the door carrying Tabitha, there came a dreadful rending sound, and one of the walls opened, letting in the light.

All fled forth, Thomas still in his surplice and his soul filled with bitterness, for as he went it came into his mind that this must be a farewell to that cherished church reared with so much love, cost and labour.

Outside the building on a patch of higher land, an upthrown plateau of rock, where presently all gathered beyond the reach of the waters, stood Menzi and Tabitha. Thomas looked at him and said:

'Doubtless you think that your spells have worked well, Witch-doctor, for see the ruin about us. Yet I hold otherwise, and say, "Wait till the end!" To set a rock rolling down a hill is easy for those who have the strength. But who knows on whom it will fall at last?'

'You speak foolishly, Teacher,' answered Menzi. 'I do not think that my spells have worked well, for something stronger than I am has spoiled them. Mayhap it is you, Teacher, or the

*Great-Great* whom you serve in your own fashion. I do not know, but I pray you to remember that long since on the smoke of my magic fire I showed you what would come about if you re-built the Heaven-house upon this place. But you said I was a cheat and would not be warned. Therefore things have gone as the Spirits appointed that they should go. Your Christians made me gifts and asked me to bring rain and it has come in plenty, and with it other things, more than you asked. Look,' and he pointed downwards.

The church was falling. Its last foundations were washed away. Down it came with a mighty crash, to melt into the flood that presently filled the place where it had been. Its collapse and the noise of it were terrible, so terrible that the Christians gathered on the rock uttered a heart-rending wail of woe. The spire, being built upon a deeper bed because of its weight, stood longer than the rest of the fabric, but presently it went also.

Thrice it seemed to bow towards them, then it fell like a child's castle. Reckoning its height with his eye, Thomas saw that it could not reach them where they stood, and so did the others, therefore no one stirred. As the tower collapsed the clock sounded the first stroke of the hour, then suddenly became silent for ever and vanished beneath the waters, a mass of broken metal.

But the bell on which it had struck was hurled forward by the sway of the fall like a stone from a sling. It sped towards them through the air, a great dark object. Men ran this way and that, so that it fell upon the rock where none stood. It fell; it flew to pieces like an exploding shell, and its fragments hurtled over them with a screaming sound. Yet as it chanced the tongue or clapper of it took a lower course, perhaps because it was heavier, and rushing onwards like a thrown spear, struck Menzi full upon the chest, crushing in his breast bone.

They bore him up to the mission-house, since there was nowhere else whither he could be taken. Here they laid him on a bed, leaving the woman, Ivana, to watch him, for they had no skill to deal with such injuries as his. Indeed, they thought him dead.

For a long while Menzi lay senseless, but after night had fallen his mind returned to him and he bade Ivana bring Tabitha to him, Tabitha and no one else. If she could not or would not come, then Ivana must bring no one else, for if she did he would curse her and die at once.

There were discussions and remonstrances, but in the end Tabitha was allowed to go, for after all a fellow-creature was dying, and this was his last wish. She came, and Menzi received her smiling. Yes, he smiled and saluted her with shaking but uplifted arm, naming her *Inkosikazi* and *Umame*, or Mother.

'Welcome, Maiden Imba. Welcome, Little Flower,' he said. 'I wish to say good-bye to you and to bless you; also to endow you with my Spirit, that it may guard you throughout your life till you are as I am. I have hated some of the others, but I have always loved you, Little Flower.'

'And I have loved you too, Menzi,' said Tabitha, with a sob.

'I know, I know! We witch-doctors read hearts. But do not weep, Little Flower. Why should you for such as I, a black man, a mere savage cheat, as your father named me? Yet I have not been altogether a cheat, O Imba, though sometimes I used tricks like other doctors, for I have a strength of my own which your white people will never understand, because they are too young to understand. It only comes to the old folk who have been since the beginning of the world, and remain as they were at the beginning. I have been wicked, Little Flower, according to your white law. I have killed men and done many other things that are according to the law of my own people, and by that law I look for judgment. Yet, O Imba, I will say this—that

LITTLE FLOWER 89

I believe your law to be higher and better than my law. Has it not been shown to-day, since of all that were gathered on the rock yonder I alone was struck down and in the hour of my victory? The strongest law must be the best law, is it not so? Tell me, Little Flower, would it please you if I died a Christian?'

'Yes, very much,' said Tabitha, fixing upon this point at once and by instinct avoiding all the other very doubtful disputations. 'I will bring my father.'

'Nay, nay, Little Flower. Your father, the Teacher Tombool, swore in his wrath that he would not come to visit me even if I lay dying, and now that I am dying he shall keep his oath and repent of it day by day till he too is dying. If I am to die a Christian, you must make me one this moment; *you* and no other. Otherwise I go hence a heathen as I have lived. If you bring your father here I will die at once before he can touch me, as I have power to do.'

Then Tabitha, who although so young had strength and understanding and knew, if she thwarted him, that Menzi would do as he threatened, took water and made a certain Sign upon the brow of that old witch-doctor, uttering also certain words that she had often heard used in church at baptisms.

Perhaps she was wrong; perhaps she transgressed and took too much upon her. Still, being by nature courageous, she ran the risk and did these things as afterwards Ivana testified to the followers of Menzi.

'Thank you, Little Flower,' said Menzi. 'I do not suppose that this Christian magic will do me any good, but that you wished it is enough. It will be a rope to tie us together, Little Flower. Also I have another thought. When it is known that I became a Christian at the last then, if *you* bid them, Little Flower, the "heathen-herd" will follow where the bull Menzi went before them. They are but broken sherds and scorched sticks' (i.e. rubbish) 'but they will follow and that will please you, Little Flower, and your father also.'

Here Menzi's breath failed, but recovering it, he continued:

'Hearken! O Imba! I give my people into your hand; now let your hand bend the twig as you would have it grow. Make them Christian if you will, or leave them heathen if you will; I care nothing. They are yours to drive upon whatever path you choose to set their feet, *yours*, O Imba, not Tombool's. Also, I, who lack heirs, give you my cattle, all of them. Ivana, make known my words, and with them the curse of Menzi, the King's child, the *Umazisi*, the Seer, on any who dare to disobey. Say to those of my House and to my people that henceforth the Maiden Imba is their lady and their mother.'

Again he paused a little, then went on:

'Now I charge my Spirit to watch over you, Little Flower, till you die and we come to talk over these matters otherwhere, and my Spirit as it departs tells me that it will watch well, and that you will be a very happy woman, Little Flower.'

He shut his eyes and lay still a while. Then he opened them again and said:

'O Imba, tell your father, the Teacher Tombool, from me that he does not understand us black people, whom he thinks so common, as you understand us, Little Flower, and that he would be wise to go to minister to white ones.'

After this, once more he smiled at Tabitha and then shut his eyes again for the last time, and that was the end of the witch-doctor Menzi.

It may be added that after he had rebuilt the church for the second time, and numbered all the 'Menzi-herd' among his congregation, which he did now that 'the bull of the herd' was dead, as Menzi had foretold that he would, if Tabitha, whom he had 'wrapped with his blanket,' decreed it, Thomas took the sage advice of his departed enemy.

Now, in the after years, he is the must respected if somewhat feared bishop of white settlers in a remote Dominion of the Crown.

Thomas to-day knows more than he used to know, but one thing he has never learned, namely that it was the hand of a maid, yes, the little hidden hand of Tabitha, that drove all 'Menzi's herd' into the gates of the 'Heavenly Kraal,' as some of them named his church.

For Tabitha knew when to be silent. Perhaps the Kaffirs, whose minds she could read as an open book, taught her this; or perhaps it was one of the best gifts to her of old Menzi's 'Spirit', into whose care he passed her with so much formality.

This is the story of the great fight between Thomas Bull the missionary and Menzi the witch-doctor, who was led by his love of a little child whither he never wished to go; not for his own soul's sake, but just because of that little child.

Menzi did not care about his soul, but, being so strange a man, for some reason that he never explained, for Tabitha, his 'Little Flower,' he cared very much indeed. That was why he became a Christian at the last, since in his darkened, spell-bound heart he believed that if he did not, when she too 'went down' he would never find her again.

# 3

## THE BLUE CURTAINS

In his regiment familiarly they called him 'Bottles,' nobody quite knew why. It was, however, rumoured that he had been called 'Bottles' at Harrow on account of the shape of his nose. Not that his nose was particularly like a bottle, but at the end of it was round and large and thick. In reality, however, the sobriquet was more ancient than that, for it had belonged to the hero of this story from babyhood. Now, when a man has a nickname, it generally implies two things: first, that he is good-tempered, and, secondly, that he is a good fellow. Bottles, *alias* John George Peritt, of a regiment it is unnecessary to name, amply justified both these definitions, for a kindlier-tempered or better fellow never breathed. But unless a thick round nose, a pair of small light-coloured eyes, set under bushy brows, and a large but not badly shaped mouth can be said to constitute beauty, he was not beautiful. On the other hand, however, he was big and well-formed, and a pleasant-mannered if a rather silent companion.

Many years ago Bottles was in love; all the regiment knew it, he was so very palpably and completely in love. Over his bed in his tidy quarters hung the photograph of a young lady who was known to be *the* young lady; which, when the regiment, individually and collectively, happened to see it, left no doubt in its mind as to their comrade's taste. It was evident even from that badly-coloured photograph that Miss Madeline Spenser had the makings of a lovely figure and a pair of wonderful eyes. It was said, however, that she had not a sixpence; and as our hero had but very few, the married ladies of the battalion used frequently to speculate how Mr. Peritt would 'manage' when it came to matrimony.

At this date the regiment was quartered in Maritzburg, Natal, but its term of foreign service had expired, and it expected to be ordered home immediately.

One morning Bottles had been out buck hunting with the scratch pack kept in those days by the garrison at Maritzburg. The run had been a good one, and after a seven or eight-mile gallop over the open country they had actually killed their buck—a beautiful Oribe. This was a thing that did not often happen, and Bottles returned filled with joy and pride with the buck fastened behind his saddle, for he was whip to the pack. The hounds had met at dawn, and it was nine o'clock or so, when, as he was riding hot and tired up the shadier side of broad and dusty Church Street, a gun fired at the Fort beyond Government House announced the arrival of the English mail.

With a beaming smile—for to him the English mail meant one if not two letters from Madeline, and possibly the glad news of sailing orders—he pushed on to his quarters, tubbed and dressed, and then went down to the mess-house for breakfast, expecting to find the letters delivered. But the mail was a heavy one, and he had ample time to eat his breakfast, also to sit and smoke a pipe upon the pleasant verandah under the shade of the bamboos and camellia bushes before the orderly arrived with the bag. Bottles went at once into the room that opened on to the veranda and stood by calmly, not being given to betraying his emotions, while slowly and clumsily the mess sergeant sorted the letters. At last he got his packet—it only consisted of some newspapers and a single letter—and went away back to his seat on the veranda, feeling rather disappointed, for he had expected to hear from his only brother as well as from his lady-love. Having relit his pipe—for he was of a slow and deliberate mind, and it rather enhances a pleasure to defer it a little—and settled himself in the big chair opposite the camellia bush just now covered with sealing-wax-like blooms, he opened his letter and read:—

'My dear George—'

'Good heavens!' he thought to himself, 'what can be the matter? She always calls me "Darling Bottles!"'

'My dear George,' he began again, 'I hardly know how to begin this letter—I can scarcely see the paper for crying, and when I think of you reading it out in that horrid country it makes me cry more than ever. There! I may as well get it out at once, for it does not improve by keeping—it is all over between you and me, my dear, dear old Bottles.'

'All over!' he gasped to himself.

'I hardly know how to tell the miserable story,' went on the letter, 'but as it must be told I suppose I had better begin from the beginning. A month ago I went with my father and my aunt to the Hunt Ball at Atherton, and there I met Sir Alfred Croston, a middle-aged gentleman, who danced with me several times. I did not care about him much, but he made himself very agreeable, and when I got home aunt—you know her nasty way—congratulated me on my conqueSt Well, next day he came to call, and papa asked him to stop to dinner, and he took me in, and before he went away he told me that he was coming to stop at the George Inn to fish for trout in the lake. After that he came here every day, and whenever I went out walking he always met me, and really was kind and nice. At last one day he asked me to marry him, and I was very angry and told him that I was engaged to a gentleman in the army, who was in South Africa. He laughed, and said South Africa was a long way off, and I hated him for it. That evening papa and aunt set on me—you know they neither of them liked our engagement—and told me that our affair was perfectly silly, and that I must be mad to refuse such an offer. And so it went on, for he would not take "no" for an answer; and at last, dear, I had to give in, for they gave me no peace, and papa implored me to consent for his sake. He said the marriage would be the making of him, and now I suppose I am engaged. Dear, dear George, don't be angry with me, for it is not my fault, and I suppose after all we could not have got married, for we have so little money. I do love you, but I can't help myself. I hope you won't forget me, or marry anybody else—at least, not just at present—for I cannot bear to think about it. Write to me and tell me you won't forget me, and that you are not angry with me. Do you want your letters back? If you burn mine that will do. Good-bye, dear! If you only knew what I suffer! It is all very well to talk like aunt does about settlements and diamonds, but they can't make up to me for you. Good-bye, dear, I cannot write any more because my head aches so.—Ever yours,

'Madeline Spenser.'

When George Peritt, *alias* Bottles, had finished reading and re-reading this letter, he folded it up neatly and put it, after his methodical fashion, into his pocket. Then he sat and stared at the red camellia blooms before him, that somehow looked as indistinct and misty as though they were fifty yards off instead of so many inches.

'It is a great blow,' he said to himself. 'Poor Madeline! How she must suffer!'

Presently he rose and walked—rather unsteadily, for he felt much upset—to his quarters, and, taking a sheet of notepaper, wrote the following letter to catch the outgoing mail:—

> 'My dear Madeline,—I have got your letter putting an end to our engagement. I don't want to dwell on myself when you must have so much to suffer, but I must say that it has been, and is, a great blow to me. I have loved you for so many years, ever since we were babies, I think; it does seem hard to lose you now after all. I thought that when we got home I might get the adjutancy of a militia regiment, and that we might have been married. I think we might have managed on five hundred a year, though perhaps I have no right to expect you to give up comforts and luxuries to which you are accustomed; but I am afraid that when one is in love one is apt to be selfish. However, all that is done with now, as, of course, putting everything else aside, I could not think of standing in your way in life. I love you much too well for that, dear Madeline, and you are too beautiful and delicate to be the wife of a poor subaltern with little beside his pay. I can honestly say that I hope you will be happy. I don't ask you to think of me too often, as that might make you less so, but perhaps sometimes when you are quiet you will spare your old lover a thought or two, because I am sure nobody could care for you more than I do. You need not be afraid that I shall forget you or marry anybody else. I shall do neither the one nor the other. I must close this now to catch the

mail; I don't know that there is anything more to say. It is a hard trial—very; but it is no good being weak and giving way, and it consoles me to think that you are "bettering yourself" as the servants say. Good-bye, dear Madeline. May God bless you, is now and ever my earnest prayer.

'J. G. Peritt.'

Scarcely was this letter finished and hastily dispatched when a loud voice was heard calling, 'Bottles, Bottles, my boy, come rejoice with me; the orders have come—we sail in a fortnight;' followed by the owner of the voice, another subaltern, and our hero's bosom friend. 'Why, you don't seem very elated,' said he of the voice, noting his friend's dejected and somewhat dazed appearance.

'No—that is, not particularly. So you sail in a fortnight, do you?'

'"You sail?" What do you mean? Why, we *all* sail, of course, from the colonel down to the drummer-boy.'

'I don't think that I—I am going to sail, Jack,' was the hesitating answer.

'Look here, old fellow, are you off your head, or have you been liquoring up, or what?'

'No—that is, I don't think so; certainly not the first—the second, I mean.'

'Then what do you mean?'

'I mean that, in short, I am sending in my papers. I like this climate—I, in short, am going to take to farming.'

'Sending in your papers! Going to take to farming! And in this God-forsaken hole, too. You *must* be screwed.'

'No, indeed. It is only ten o'clock.'

'And how about getting married, and the girl you are engaged to, and whom you are looking forward so much to seeing. Is she going to take to farming?'

Bottles winced visibly.

'No, you see—in short, we have put an end to that. I am not engaged now.'

'Oh, indeed,' said the friend, and awkwardly departed.

Twelve years have passed since Bottles sent in his papers, and in twelve years many things happen. Amongst them recently it had happened that our hero's only and elder brother had, owing to an unexpected development of consumption among the expectant heirs, tumbled into a baronetcy and eight thousand a year, and Bottles himself into a modest but to him most ample fortune of as many hundred. When the news reached him he was the captain of a volunteer corps engaged in one of the numerous Basuto wars in the Cape Colony. He served the campaign out, and then, in obedience to his brother's entreaties and a natural craving to see his native land, after an absence of nearly fourteen years, resigned his commission and returned to England.

Thus it came to pass that the next scene of this little history opens, not upon the South African veld, or in a whitewashed house in some half-grown, hobbledehoy colonial town, but in a set of the most comfortable chambers in the Albany, the local and appropriate habitation of the bachelor brother aforesaid, Sir Eustace Peritt.

In a very comfortable arm-chair in front of a warm fire (for the month is November) sits the Bottles of old days—bigger, uglier, shyer than ever, and in addition, disfigured by an assegai wound through the cheek. Opposite to him, and peering at him occasionally with fond curiosity through an eyeglass, is his brother, a very different stamp of man. Sir Eustace Peritt is a well-preserved, London-looking gentleman, of apparently any age between thirty and fifty. His eye is so bright, his figure so well preserved, that to judge from appearances alone you would put him down to the former age. But when you come to know him so as to be able to measure his consummate knowledge of the world, and to have the opportunity of reflecting upon the good-natured but profound cynicism which pleasantly pervades his talk as absolutely as the flavour of lemon pervades rum punch, you would be inclined to assign his natal day to a much earlier date. In reality he was forty, neither more nor less, and had both preserved his youthful appearance and gained the mellowness of his experience by a judicious use of the opportunities of life.

'Well, my dear George,' said Sir Eustace, addressing his brother—determined to take this occasion of meeting after so long a time to be rid of the nickname 'Bottles,' which he hated—'I haven't had such a pleasure for years.'

'As—as what?'

'As meeting you again, of course. When I saw you on the vessel I knew you at once. You have not changed at all, unless expansion can be called a change.'

'Nor have you, Eustace, unless contraction can be called a change. Your waist used to be bigger, you know.'

'Ah, George, I drank beer in those days; it is one of things of which I have lived to see the folly. In fact, there are not many things of which I have not lived to see the folly.'

'Except living itself, I suppose?'

'Exactly—except living. I have no wish to follow the example of our poor cousins,' he answered with a sigh, 'to whose considerate behaviour, however,' he added, brightening, 'we owe our present improved position.' Then came a pause.

'Fourteen years is a long time, George; you must have had a rough time of it.'

'Yes, pretty rough. I have seen a good deal of irregular service, you know.'

'And never got anything out of it, I suppose?'

'Oh, yes; I have got my bread and butter, which is all I am worth.'

Sir Eustace looked at his brother doubtfully through his eyeglass. 'You are modest,' he said; 'that does not do. You must have a better opinion of yourself if you want to get on in the world.'

'I don't want to get on. I am quite content to earn a living, and I am modest because I have seen so many better men fare worse.'

'But now you need not earn a living any more. What do you propose to do? Live in town? I can set you going in a very good lot. You will be quite a lion with that hole in your cheek—by the way, you must tell me the story. And then, you see, if anything happens to me you stand in for the title and estates. That will be quite enough to float you.'

Bottles writhed uneasily in his chair. 'Thank you, Eustace; but really I must ask you—in short, I don't want to be floated or anything of the sort. I would rather go back to South Africa and my volunteer corps. I would indeed. I hate strangers, and society, and all that sort of thing. I'm not fit for it like you.'

'Then what do you mean to do—get married and live in the country?'

Bottles coloured a little through his sun-tanned skin—a fact that did not escape the eyeglass of his observant brother. 'No, I am not going to get married, certainly not.'

'By the way,' said Sir Eustace carelessly, 'I saw your old flame, Lady Croston, yesterday, and told her you were coming home. She makes a charming widow.'

'*What!*' ejaculated his brother, slowly raising himself out of his chair in astonishment. 'Is her husband dead?'

'Dead? Yes, died a year ago, and a good riddance too. He appointed me one of his executors; I am sure I don't know why, for we never liked each other. I think he was the most disagreeable fellow I ever knew. They say he gave his wife a roughish time of it occasionally. Serve her right, too.'

'Why did it serve her right?'

Sir Eustace shrugged his shoulders.

'When a heartless girl jilts the fellow she is engaged to in order to sell herself to an elderly beast, I think she deserves all she gets. This one did not get half enough; indeed, she has made a good thing of it—better than she expected.'

His brother sat down again before he answered in a constrained voice, 'Don't you think you are rather hard on her, Eustace?'

'Hard on her? No, not a bit of it. Of all the worthless women that I know, I think Madeline Croston is the most worthless. Look how she treated you.'

'Eustace,' broke in his brother almost sharply, 'if you don't mind, I wish you would not talk of her like that to me. I can't—in short, I don't like it.'

Sir Eustace's eyeglass dropped out of Sir Eustace's eye—he had opened it so wide to stare at his brother. 'Why, my dear fellow,' he ejaculated, 'you don't mean to tell me you still care for that woman?'

His brother twisted his great form about uncomfortably in the low chair as he answered, 'I don't know, I'm sure, about caring for her, but I don't like to hear you say such things about her.'

Sir Eustace whistled softly. 'I am sorry if I offended you, old fellow,' he said. 'I had no idea that it was still a sore point with you. You must be a faithful people in South Africa. Here the "holy feelings of the heart" are shorter lived. We wear out several generations of them in twelve years.'

Bottles did not go to bed till late that night. Long after Sir Eustace—who, always careful of his health, never stopped up late if he could avoid it—had vanished, yawning, his brother sat smoking pipe after pipe and thinking. He had sat many times in the same way on a wagon-box in the African veld, or up where the moonlight turned the falls of the Zambesi into a rushing cataract of silver, or alone in his tent when all the camp was sleeping round him. It was a habit of this queer, silent man to sit and think for hours at night, and arose to a great extent from an incapacity to sleep, that was the weak point in his constitution.

As for his meditations, they were various, but mostly the outcome of a curious speculative side to his nature, which he never revealed to the outside world. Dreams of a happiness of which heretofore his hard life had given him no glimpse; semi-mystical, religious meditations upon the great unknown around us; and grand schemes for the regeneration of mankind—all formed part of them.

But there was one central thought, the fixed star of his mind, round which all the others continually revolved, taking their light and colour from it, and that was the thought of Madeline Croston, the woman to whom he had been engaged. Years and years had passed since he had seen her face, and yet it was always present to him. Beyond the occasional mention of her name in some society paper—several of which, by the way, he took in for years and conscientiously searched on the chance of finding it—till this evening he had never even seen it or heard it spoken; and yet with all the tenacity of his strong, deep nature he clung to her dear memory. That she had left him to marry another man weighed as nothing in the balance of his love. Once she had loved him, and thereby he was repaid for the devotion of his life. He had no ambitions. Madeline had been his great ambition; and when that had fallen, all the others had fallen with it, even to the duSt He simply did his duty, whatever it might be, as well as in him lay, without fear of blame or hope of praise—shunning men, and never, if he could avoid it, speaking to a woman, content to earn his livelihood, and for the rest rendered colourless by his secret and pathetic passion.

And now it appeared that Madeline was a widow, which meant—and his heart beat fast at the thought—that she was a free woman. Madeline was a free woman, and he was within a few minutes' walk of her. No thousands of miles of ocean rolled between them now. He rose, went to the table, and consulted a Red book that lay on it. There was the address—a house in Grosvenor Street. Overcome by an uncontrollable impulse, he went out of the room. Going to his own he found his mackintosh and a round hat, and softly left the house. It was then past two in the morning, pouring with rain, and blowing hard.

He had been a little in London as a lad and remembered the main thoroughfares, so had no great difficulty in finding his way up Piccadilly till he came to Park Lane, into which the Red book told him Grosvenor Square opened. But to find Grosvenor Street itself was a more difficult matter, and at such a time on such a night there was naturally nobody to ask—least of all a policeman. At last he found it, and hurried on down the street with a quickening pulse. What he was hurrying to he could not tell, but that over-mastering impulse forced him on quicker and quicker yet.

Suddenly he halted, and examined the number of one of the houses by the faint and struggling light from the nearest lamp. It was *her* house; now there was nothing between them but a few feet of space and fourteen inches of brickwork. He crossed over to the other side of the street, and looked up at the house, but could scarcely make it out through the driving rain. There was no light in the house, and no sign of life about the street. But there were both light and life in the heart of this watcher. All the pulses of his blood were astir, keeping time with the commotion of his mind. He stood there in the shadow, gazing at the murky house, heedless of the bitter wind and pelting rain, and felt his life and spirit pass out of his control into an unknown dominion. The storm that raged around him was nothing to the convulsion of his inner self in that hour of madness, which was yet happiness. Yet as it had arisen thus suddenly, so with equal swiftness it died away, and left him standing there with a chill sense of folly in his mind and of the bitter weather in his body; for on such a night a mackintosh and a dress coat were not adapted to keep the most ardent lover warm. He shivered, and turning, made his way back to Albany, feeling heartily ashamed of himself and his midnight expedition, and heartily glad that no one knew of it except himself.

On the following day Bottles—for convenience' sake we still call him by his old nickname—was obliged to see a lawyer with reference to the money which he had inherited, and to search for a box which had gone astray aboard the steamer; also to buy a tall hat, such as he had not worn for fourteen years; so that between one thing and another it was half-past four before he got back to the Albany. Here he donned the new hat, which did not fit very well, and a new black coat which fitted so well that it seemed to cut into his large frame in every possible direction, and departed, furiously struggling with a pair of gloves, also new, for Grosvenor Street.

A quarter of an hour's walk, for he knew the road this time, brought him to the house. Glancing for a while at the spot where he had stood on the previous night, he walked up the steps and pulled the bell. Though he looked bold enough outwardly—indeed, rather imposing than otherwise—with his broad shoulders and the great scar on his bronzed face, his breast was full of terrors. In these, however, he had not much time to indulge, for a footman, still decked in the trappings of vicarious grief, opened the door with the most startling promptitude, and he was ushered upstairs into a small but richly furnished room.

Madeline was not in the room, though to judge from the lace handkerchief lying on the floor by a low chair, and the open novel on a little wicker table alongside, she had not left it long. The footman departed, saying, in a magnificent undertone, that 'her ladyship' should be informed, and left our hero to enjoy his sensations. Being one of those people whom suspense of any sort makes fidgety, he employed himself in looking at the pictures and china, even going so far as to walk to a pair of very heavy blue velvet curtains that apparently communicated with another room, and peep through them at a much larger apartment of which the furniture was done up in ghostly-looking bags.

Retreating from this melancholy sight, finally he took up a position on the hearthrug and waited. Would she be angry with him for coming? he wondered. Would it recall things she had rather forget? But perhaps she had already forgotten them—it was so long ago. Would she be very much changed? Perhaps he should not know her. Perhaps—but here he happened to lift his eyes, and there, standing between the two blue velvet curtains, was Madeline, now a woman in the full splendour of a remarkable beauty, and showing as yet, at any rate in that dull November twilight, no traces of her years. There she stood, her large dark eyes fixed upon him with a look of wistful curiosity, her shapely lips just parted to speak, and her bosom gently heaving, as though with trouble.

Poor Bottles! One look was enough. There was no chance of his attaining the blessed haven of disillusionment. In five seconds he was farther out to sea than ever. When she knew that he had seen her she dropped her eyes a little—he saw the long curved lashes appear against her cheek, and moved forward.

'How do you do?' she said softly, extending her slim, cool hand.

He took the hand and shook it, but for the life of him could think of nothing to say. Not one of the little speeches he had prepared would come into his mind. Yet the desperate necessity of saying something forced itself upon him.

'How do you do?' he ejaculated with a jerk. 'It—it's very cold, isn't it?'

This remark was such an utter and ludicrous *fiasco* that Lady Croston could not choose but laugh a little.

'I see,' she said, 'that you have not got over your shyness.'

'It is a long while since we met,' he blurted out.

'I am very glad to see you,' was her simple answer. 'Now sit down and talk to me; tell me all about yourself. Stop; before you begin—how very curious it is! Do you know I dreamed about you last night—such a curious, painful dream. I dreamed that I was asleep in my room—which indeed I was—and that it was blowing a gale and raining in torrents—which I believe it was also—so there is nothing very wonderful about that. But now comes the odd part. I dreamed that you were standing out in the rain and wind and yet looking at me as though you saw me. I could not see your face because you were in the dark, but I knew it was you. Then I woke up with a start. It was a most vivid dream. And now to-day you have come to see me after all these years.'

He shifted his legs uneasily. Considering the facts of the case, her dream frightened him, which was not strange. Fortunately, at that moment the impressive footman arrived with the tea-things and asked whether he should light the lamps.

'No,' said Lady Croston; 'put some wood on the fire.' She knew that she looked her very best in those half-lights.

Then, when she had given him his tea, delighting him by remembering that he did not like sugar, she fell to drawing him out about the wild life he had been leading.

'By the way,' she said presently, 'perhaps you can tell me—a few days ago I bought a book for my boy'—she had two children—'all about brave deeds and that sort of thing, and in it there was a story of a volunteer officer in South Africa (the name was not mentioned) which interested me very much. Did you ever hear of it? It was this: The officer was in command of a fort containing a force that was operating against a native chief. While he was away the chief sent a flag of truce down to the fort, which was fired on by some of the volunteers in the fort, because there was a man among the truce party against whom they had a spite. Just afterwards the officer returned, and was very angry that such a thing had been done by Englishmen, whose duty it was, he said, to teach all the world what honour meant.

'Now comes the brave part of the story. Without saying any more, and notwithstanding the entreaties of his men, who knew that in all probability he was going to a death by torture, for he was so brave that the natives had set a great price upon him, wishing to kill him and use his body for medicine, which they thought would make them as brave as he was, that officer rode out far away into the mountains with only an interpreter and a white handkerchief, till he came to the chief's stronghold. But when the natives saw him coming, holding up his white handkerchief, they did not fire at him as his men had fired at them, because they were so astonished at his bravery that they thought he must be mad or inspired. So he came straight on to the walls of the stronghold, called to the chief and begged his pardon for what had happened, and then rode away again unharmed. Shortly afterwards, the chief, having captured some of the officer's volunteers, whom in the ordinary course of affairs he would have tortured to death, sent them back again untouched, with a message to the effect that he would show the English officer that he was not the only man who could behave "like a gentleman." I should like to know that man. Do you know who he was?'

Bottles looked uncomfortable, as well he might, for it was an incident in his own career; but her praise and enthusiasm sent a flush of pride into his face.

'I believe it was some fellow in the Basuto War,' he said, prevaricating with peculiar awkwardness.

'Oh, then it *is* a true story?'

'Yes—that is, it is partially true. There was nothing heroic about it. It was a necessary act if our honour as fair opponents was to continue to be worth anything.'

'But who was the man?' she asked, fixing her dark eyes on him suspiciously.

'The man!' he stammered. 'Oh, the man—well, in short—' and he stopped.

'In short, *George*,' she put in, for the first time calling him by his Christian name, 'that man was *you*, and I am so proud of you, George.'

It was very hateful to him in a way, for he loathed that kind of personal adulation, even from her. He was so intensely modest he had never even reported the incident in question; it had come out in some roundabout way. Yet he could not but feel happy that she had found him out. It was a great deal to him to have moved her, and her sparkling eyes and heaving bosom showed that she was somewhat moved.

He looked up and his eyes caught hers; the room was nearly dark now, but the bright flame from the wood the servant had put on the fire played upon her face. His eyes caught hers, and there was a look in them from which he could not escape, even if he had wished to do so. She had thrown her head back so that the coronet of her glossy hair rested upon the back of her low seat, and thus, without strain, could look straight up into his face. He had risen, and was standing by the mantelpiece. A slow, sweet smile grew upon the perfect face, and the dark eyes became soft and luminous as though they shone through tears.

In another second it had ended, as she thought that it would end and had intended that it should end. The great strong man was down—yes, down on his knees before her, one trembling hand catching at the arm of her chair, and the other clasping her tapering fingers. There was no hesitation or awkwardness about him now, the greatness of his long-pent passion inspired him, and he told her all without let or stop—all that he had suffered for her sake throughout those lonely years, all his wretched hopelessness, keeping nothing back.

Much she did not understand; such a passion as this was too deep to be fathomed by her shallow lines, too soaring for her to net in her world-straitened imagination. Once or twice even his exalted notions made her smile: it seemed ridiculous, knowing the world as she did, that any man should think thus of *any* woman. Nor, when at length he had finished, did she attempt an answer, feeling that her strength lay in silence, for she had a poor case. At least, the only argument that she used was a purely feminine one, but perfectly effective. She bent her beautiful face towards him, and he kissed it again and again.

The revulsion of feeling experienced by Bottles as he hurried back to the Albany to dress for dinner—for he was to dine with his brother at one of his clubs that night—was so extraordinary and overwhelming that it took him, figuratively speaking, off his legs. As yet his mind, so long accustomed to perpetual misfortune in this, the ruling passion of his life, could not quite grasp his luck. That he should, after all, have won back his lost Madeline seemed altogether too good to be true.

As it happened, Sir Eustace had asked one or two men to meet him, amongst them an Under-Secretary for the Colonies, who, having to prepare for a severe cross-examination in the

House upon South African affairs, had jumped at the opportunity of sucking the brains of a man thoroughly acquainted with the subject. But the expectant Under-Secretary was destined to meet with a grievous disappointment, for out of Bottles came no good thing. For the most part of the dinner he sat silent, only speaking when directly addressed, and then answering so much at random that the Under-Secretary quickly came to the conclusion that Sir Eustace's brother was either a fool or that he had drunk too much.

Sir Eustace himself saw that his brother's taciturnity had spoilt his little dinner, and his temper was not improved thereby. He was not accustomed to have his dinners spoiled, and felt that, so far as the Under-Secretary was concerned, he had put himself into a false position.

'My dear George,' he said in a tone of bland exasperation when they had got back to the Albany, 'I wonder what can be the matter with you? I told Atherleigh that you would be able to post him up thoroughly about all this Bechuana mess, and he could not get a word out of you.'

His brother absently filled his pipe before he answered:

'The Bechuanas? Oh, yes, I know all about them. I lived among them for a year.'

'Then why on earth didn't you tell him what you knew? You put me in rather a false position.'

'I am very sorry, Eustace,' he answered humbly. 'I will go and see him if you like, and explain the thing to him to-morrow. The fact of the matter is, I was thinking of something else.'

Sir Eustace interrogated him with a look.

'I was thinking,' he went on slowly, 'about Mad—about Lady Croston.'

'Oh!'

'I went to see her this afternoon, and I think, I hope, that I am going to marry her.'

If Bottles expected that this great news would be received by his elder brother as such news ought to be received—with congratulatory rejoicing—he was destined to be disappointed.

'Good heavens!' ejaculated Sir Eustace shortly, letting his eyeglass drop.

'Why do you say that, Eustace?' Bottles asked uneasily.

'Because—because,' answered his brother in the emphatic tone which was his equivalent for strong language, 'you must be mad to think of such a thing.'

'Why must I be mad?'

'Because you, still a young man, with all your life before you, deliberately propose to tie yourself up to a middle-aged and *passee* woman—she is extremely *passee* by daylight, let me tell you—who has already treated you like a dog, and is burdened with a couple of children, and who, if she marries again, will bring you very little except her luxurious tastes. But I expected this. I thought she would try to catch you with those languishing black eyes of hers. You are not the first; I know her of old.'

'If,' said his brother, rising in dudgeon, 'you are going to abuse Madeline to me, I think I had better say good night, for we shall quarrel—which I would not do for anything.'

Sir Eustace shrugged his shoulders. 'Those whom the gods wish to destroy they first make mad,' he muttered, as he lit his hand candle. 'This is what comes of a course of South Africa.'

But Sir Eustace was an amenable man. His favourite motto was 'Live and let live'; and having given the matter his best consideration during the lengthy process of shaving himself on the following morning, he came to the conclusion, reluctantly enough it must be owned, that it was evident that his brother meant to have his own way, and therefore the best thing to be done was to fall in with his views and trust to the chapter of accidents to bring the thing to naught. Sir Eustace, for all his apparent worldliness and cynicism, was a good fellow at heart, and cherished a warm affection for his awkward, taciturn brother. He also cherished a great dislike for Lady Croston, whose character he thoroughly understood. He saw a good deal of her, it is true, because he happened to be one of the executors of her husband's will; and since he had come into the baronetcy it had struck him that she had developed a considerable partiality for his society.

The idea of a marriage between his brother and his brother's old flame was in every way distasteful to him. In the first place, under her husband's will, Madeline would bring, comparatively speaking, relatively little with her should she marry again. That was one objection. Another, and still more forcible one from Sir Eustace's point of view, was that at her time of life she was not likely to present the house of Peritt with an heir. Now, Sir Eustace had not the slightest intention of marrying. Matrimony was, he considered, an excellent institution, and necessary to the carrying on of the world in a respectable manner, but it was not one with which he was anxious to identify himself. Therefore, if his brother married at all, it was his earnest desire that the union should bring children to inherit the title and estates. Prominent above both these excellent reasons, stood his intense distrust and dislike of the lady.

Needs must, however, when the devil (by whom he understood Madeline) drives. He was not going to quarrel with his only brother and presumptive heir because he chose to marry a woman who was not to his taste. So he shrugged his shoulders—having finished his shaving and his reflections together—and determined to put the best possible face on his disappointment.

'Well, George,' he said to his brother at breakfast, 'so you are going to marry Lady Croston?'

Bottles looked up surprised. 'Yes, Eustace,' he answered, 'if she will marry me.'

Sir Eustace glanced at him. 'I thought the affair was settled,' he said.

Bottles rubbed his big nose reflectively as he answered, 'Well, no. I don't think that marriage was mentioned. But I suppose she means to marry me. In short, I don't see how she could mean anything else.'

Sir Eustace breathed more freely, guessing what had taken place. So there was as yet no actual engagement.

'When are you going to see her again?'

'To-morrow. She is engaged all to-day.'

His brother took out a pocket-book and consulted it. 'Then I am more fortunate than you are,' he said; 'I have an appointment with Lady Croston this evening after dinner. Don't look jealous, old fellow, it is only about some executor's business. I think I told you that I am one of her husband's executors, blessings on his memory. She is a peculiar woman, your *inamorata*, and swears that she won't trust her lawyers, so I have to do all the dirty work myself, worse luck. You had better come too.'

'Shan't I be in the way?' asked Bottles doubtfully, struggling feebly against the bribe.

'It is evident, my dear fellow, that you cannot be *de trop*. I shall present my papers for signature and vanish. You ought to be infinitely obliged to me for giving you such a chance. We will consider that settled. We will dine together, and go round to Grosvenor Street afterwards.'

Bottles agreed. Could he have seen the little scheme that was dawning in his brother's brain, perhaps he would not have assented so readily.

When her old lover went away reluctantly to dress for dinner on the previous day, Madeline Croston sat down to have a good think, and the result was not entirely satisfactory. It had been very pleasant to see him, and his passionate declaration of enduring love thrilled her through and through, and even woke an echo in her own breaSt It made her proud to think that this man, who, notwithstanding his ugliness and awkwardness, was yet, her instinct told her, worth half a dozen smart London fashionables, still loved her and had never ceased to love her. Poor Bottles! she had been very fond of him once. They had grown up together, and it really gave her some cruel hours when a sense of what she owed to herself and her family had forced her to discard him.

She remembered, as she sat there this evening, how at the time she had wondered if it was worth it—if life would not be brighter and happier if she made up her mind to fight through it by her honest lover's side. Well, she could answer that question now. It had been well worth it. She had not liked her husband, it is true; but on the whole she had enjoyed a good time and plenty of money, and the power that money brings. The wisdom of her later days had confirmed the judgment of her youth. As regards Bottles himself, she had soon got over that fancy; for years she had scarcely thought of him, till Sir Eustace told her that he was coming home, and she had that curious dream about him. Now he had come and made love to her, not in a civilised, philandering sort of a way, such as she was accustomed to, but with a passion and a fire and an utter self-abandonment which, while it thrilled her nerves with a curious sensation of mingled pleasure and pain, not unlike that she once experienced at a Spanish bull-fight when she saw a man tossed, was yet extremely awkward to deal with and rather alarming.

Now, too, the old question had come up again, and what was to be done? She had sheered him off the question that afternoon, but he would want to marry her, she felt sure of that. If she consented, what were they to live on? Her own juncture, in the event of her re-marriage, would be cut down to a thousand a year—she had four now, and was pinched on that; and as for Bottles, she knew what he had—eight hundred, for Sir Eustace had told her. He was next heir to the baronetcy, it was true, but Sir Eustace looked as though he would live for ever, and besides, he might marry after all.

For a few minutes Lady Croston contemplated the possibility of existing on eighteen hundred a year, and what Chancery would give her as guardian of her children in a poky house somewhere down at Kensington. Soon she realised that the thing was not to be done.

'Unless Sir Eustace will do something for him, it is very clear that we cannot be married,' she said to herself with a sigh. 'However, I need not tell him that just yet, or he will be rushing back to South Africa or something.'

Sir Eustace and his brother carried out their programme. They dined together, and about half-past nine drove round to Grosvenor Street. Here they were shown into the drawing-room by the solemn footman, who informed Sir Eustace that her ladyship was upstairs in the nursery and had left a message for him that she would be down presently.

'All right; there is no hurry,' said Sir Eustace absently, and the man went downstairs.

Bottles, being nervous, was fidgeting round the room as usual, and his brother, being very much at ease, was standing with his back to the fire, and staring about him. Presently his glance lit upon the blue velvet curtains which shut off the room they were in from the larger saloon that had not been used since Lady Croston's widowhood, and an idea which had been floating about in his brain suddenly took definite shape and form. He was a prompt man, and in another second he had acted up to that idea.

'George,' he said in a quick, low voice, 'listen to me, and for Heaven's sake don't interrupt for a minute. You know that

I do not like the idea of your marrying Lady Croston. You know that I think her worthless—no, wait a minute, don't interrupt—I am only saying what I think. You believe in her; you believe that she is in love with you and will marry you, and have good reason to believe it, have you not?'

Bottles nodded.

'Very well. Supposing that I can show you within half an hour that she is perfectly ready to marry somebody else—myself, for instance—would you still believe in her?'

Bottles turned pale. 'The thing is impossible,' he said.

'That is not the question. Would you still believe in her, and would you still marry her?'

'Great heavens! no.'

'Good. Then I tell you what I will do for you, and it will perhaps give you some idea of how deeply I feel in the matter; I will sacrifice myself.'

'Sacrifice yourself?'

'Yes. I mean that I will this very evening propose to Madeline Croston under your nose, and I bet you five pounds she accepts me.'

'Impossible,' said Bottles again. 'Besides, if she did you don't want to marry her.'

'Marry her! No, indeed. *I* am not mad. I shall have to get out of the scrape as best I can—always supposing my view of the lady is correct.'

'Excuse me,' said Bottles with a gasp, 'but I must ask you—in short, have *you* ever been on affectionate terms with Madeline?'

'Never, on my honour.'

'And yet you think she will marry you if you ask her, even after what took place with me yesterday?'

'Yes, I do.'

'Why?'

'Because, my boy,' replied Sir Eustace with a cynical smile, 'I have eight thousand a year and you have eight hundred—because I have a title and you have none. That you may happen to be the better fellow of the two will, I fear, not make up for those deficiencies.'

Bottles with a motion of his hand waved his brother's courtly compliment away, as it were, and turned on him with a set white face.

'I do not believe you, Eustace,' he said. 'Do you understand what you make out this lady to be when you say that she could kiss me and tell me that she loved me—for she did both yesterday—and promise to marry you to-day?'

Sir Eustace shrugged his shoulders. 'I think that the lady in question has done something like that before, George.'

'That was years ago and under pressure. Now, Eustace, you have made this charge; you have upset my faith in Madeline, whom I hope to marry, and I say, prove it—prove it if you can. I will stake my life you cannot.'

'Don't agitate yourself, my dear fellow; and as to betting, I would not risk more than a fiver. Now oblige me by stepping behind those velvet curtains—*a la* "School for Scandal"—and listening in perfect silence to my conversation with Lady Croston. She does not know that you are here, so she will not miss you. You can escape when you have had enough of it, for there is a door through on to the landing, and as we came up I noticed that it was ajar. Or if you like you can appear from between the curtains like an infuriated husband on the stage and play whatever *role* occasion may demand. Really the situation has a laughable side. I should enjoy it immensely if *I* were behind the curtain too. Come, in you go.'

Bottles hesitated. 'I can't hide,' he said.

'Nonsense; remember how much depends on it. All is fair in love or war. Quick; here she comes.'

Bottles grew flurried and yielded, scarcely knowing what he did. In another second he was in the darkened room behind the curtains, through the crack in which he could command the lighted scene before him, and Sir Eustace was back at his place before the fire, reflecting that in his ardour to extricate his brother from what he considered a suicidal engagement he had let himself in for a very pretty undertaking. Suppose she accepted him, his brother would be furious, and he would probably have to go abroad to get out of the lady's way; and suppose she refused him, he would look a fool.

Meanwhile the sweep, sweep of Madeline's dress as she passed down the stairs was drawing nearer, and in another instant she was in the room. She was beautifully dressed in silver-grey silk, plentifully trimmed with black lace, and cut square back and front so as to show her rounded shoulders. She wore no ornaments, being one of the few women who are able to dispense with them, unless indeed a red camellia pinned in the front of her dress can be called an ornament. Bottles, shivering with shame and doubt behind his curtain, marked that red camellia, and wondered of what it reminded him.

Then in a flash it all came back, the scene of years and years ago—the verandah in far-away Natal, with himself sitting on it, an open letter in his hand and staring with all his eyes at the camellia bush covered with bloom before him. It seemed a bad omen to him—that camellia in Madeline's bosom. Next second she was speaking.

'Oh, Sir Eustace, I owe you a thousand apologies. You must have been here for quite ten minutes, for I heard the front door bang when you came. But my poor little girl Effie is ill with a sore throat which has made her feverish, and she absolutely refused to go to sleep unless she had my hand to hold.'

'Lucky Effie,' said Sir Eustace, with his politest bow; 'I am sure I can understand her fancy.'

At the moment he was holding Madeline's hand himself, and gave emphasis to his words by communicating the gentlest possible pressure to it as he let it fall. But knowing his habits, she did not take much notice. Comparative strangers when Sir Eustace shook hands with them were sometimes in doubt whether he was about to propose to them or to make a remark upon the weather. Alas! it had always been the weather.

'I come as a man of business besides, and men of business are accustomed to being kept waiting,' he went on.

'You are really very good, Sir Eustace, to take so much trouble about my affairs.'

'It is a pleasure, Lady Croston.'

'Ah, Sir Eustace, you do not expect me to believe that,' laughed the radiant creature at his side. 'But if you only knew how I detest lawyers, and what you spare me by the trouble you take, I am sure you would not grudge me your time.'

'Do not talk of it, Lady Croston. I would do a great deal more than that for you; in fact,' here he dropped his voice a little, 'there are few things that I would not do for you, *Madeline*.'

She raised her delicate eyebrows till they looked like notes of interrogation, and blushed a little. This was quite a new style for Sir Eustace. Was he in earnest? she wondered. Impossible!

'And now for business,' he continued; 'not that there is much business; as I understand it, you have only to sign this document, which I have already witnessed, and the stock can be transferred.'

She signed the paper which he had brought in a big envelope almost without looking at it, for she was thinking of Sir Eustace's remark, and he put it back in the envelope.

'Is that all the business, Sir Eustace?' she asked.

'Yes; quite all. Now I suppose that as I have done my duty I had better go away.'

'I wish to Heaven he would!' groaned Bottles to himself

behind the curtains. He did not like his brother's affectionate little ways or Madeline's tolerance of them.

'Indeed, no; you had better sit down and talk to me—that is, if you have got nothing pleasanter to do.'

We can guess Sir Eustace's prompt reply and Madeline's smiling reception of the compliment, as she seated herself in a low chair—that same low chair she had occupied the day before.

'Now for it,' said Sir Eustace to himself. 'I wonder how George is getting on?'

'My brother tells me that he came to see you yesterday,' he began.

'Yes,' she answered, smiling again, but wondering in her heart how much he had told him.

'Do you find him much changed?'

'Not much.'

'You used to be very fond of each other once, if I remember right?' said he.

'Yes, once.'

'I often think how curious it is,' went on Sir Eustace in a reflective tone, 'to watch the various changes time brings about, especially where the affections are concerned. One sees children at the seaside making little mounds of sand, and they think, if they are very young children, that they will find them there to-morrow. But they reckon without their tide. To-morrow the sands will have swept as level as ever, and the little boys will have to begin again. It is like that with our youthful love affairs, is it not? The tide of time comes up and sweeps them away, fortunately for ourselves. Now in your case, for instance, it is, I think, a happy thing for both of you that your sandhouse did not laSt Is it not?'

Madeline sighed softly. 'Yes, I suppose so,' she answered.

Bottles, behind the curtains, rapidly reviewed the past, and came to a different conclusion.

'Well, that is all done with,' said Sir Eustace cheerfully.

Madeline did not contradict him; she did not see her way to doing so just at present.

Then came a pause.

'Madeline,' said Sir Eustace presently, in a changed voice, 'I have something to say to you.'

'Indeed, Sir Eustace,' she answered, lifting her eyebrows again in her note of interrogation manner, 'what is it?'

'It is this, Madeline—I want to ask you to be my wife.'

The blue velvet curtains suddenly gave a jump as though they were assisting at at spiritualistic *seance*.

Sir Eustace looked at the curtains with warning in his eye.

Madeline saw nothing.

'Really, Sir Eustace!'

'I dare say I surprise you,' went on this ardent lover; 'my suit may seem a sudden one, but in truth it is nothing of the sort.'

'O Lord, what a lie!' groaned the distracted Bottles.

'I thought, Sir Eustace,' murmured Madeline in her sweet low voice, 'that you told me not very long ago that you never meant to marry.'

'Nor did I, Madeline, because I thought there was no chance of my marrying you' ('which I am sure I hope there isn't,' he added to himself). 'But—but, Madeline, I love you.' ('Heaven forgive me for that!') 'Listen to me, Madeline, before you answer,' and he drew his chair closer to her own. 'I feel the loneliness of my position, and I want to get married. I think that we should suit each other very well. At our age, now that our youth is past' (he could not resist this dig, at which Madeline winced), 'probably neither of us would wish to marry anybody much our junior. I have had many opportunities lately, Madeline, of seeing the beauty of your character, and to the beauties of your person no man could be blind. I can offer you a good position, a good fortune, and myself, such as I am. Will you take me?' and he laid his hand upon hers and gazed earnestly into her eyes.

'Really, Sir Eustace,' she murmured, 'this is so very unexpected and sudden.'

'Yes, Madeline, I know it is. I have no right to take you by storm in this way, but I trust you will not allow my precipitancy to weight against me. Take a little time to think it over—a week say' ('by which time,' he reflected, 'I hope to be in Algiers.') 'Only, if you can, Madeline, tell me that I may hope.'

She made no immediate answer, but, letting her hands fall idly in her lap, looked straight before her, her beautiful eyes fixed upon vacancy, and her mind amply occupied in considering the pros and cons of the situation. Then Sir Eustace took heart of grace; bending down, he kissed the Madonna-like face. Still there was no response. Only very gently she pushed him from her, whispering:

'Yes, Eustace, I think I shall be able to tell you that you may hope.'

Bottles waited to see no more. With set teeth and flaming eyes he crept, a broken man, through the door that led on to the landing, crept down the stairs and into the hall. On the pegs were his hat and coat; he took them and passed into the street.

'I have done a disgraceful thing,' he thought, 'and I have paid for it.'

Softly as the door closed Sir Eustace heard it; and then he too left the room, murmuring, 'I shall soon come for my answer, Madeline.'

When he reached the street his brother was gone.

Sir Eustace did not go straight back to the Albany, but, calling a hansom, drove down to his club.

'Well,' he thought to himself, 'I have played a good many

curious parts in my time, but I never had to do with anything like this before. I only hope George is not much cut up. His eyes ought to be opened now. What a woman—' but we will not repeat Sir Eustace's comments upon the lady to whom he was nominally half engaged.

At the club Sir Eustace met his friend the Under-Secretary, who had just escaped from the House. Thanks to information furnished to him that morning by Bottles, who had been despatched by Sir Eustace, in a penitent mood, to the Colonial Office to see him, he had just succeeded in confusing, if not absolutely in defeating, the impertinent people who 'wanted to know.' Accordingly he was jubilant, and greeted Sir Eustace with enthusiasm, and they sat talking together for an hour or more.

Then Sir Eustace, being, as has been said, of early habits, made his way home.

In his sitting-room he found his brother smoking and contemplating the fire.

'Hullo, old fellow!' he said, 'I wish you had come to the club with me. Atherleigh was there, and is delighted with you. What you told him this morning enabled him to smash up his enemies, and as the smashing lately has been rather the other way he is jubilant. He wants you to go to see him again to-morrow. Oh, by the way, you made your escape all right. I only hope I may be as lucky. Well, what do you think of your lady-love now?'

'I think,' said Bottles slowly—'that I had rather not say what I do think.'

'Well, you are not going to marry her now, I suppose?'

'No, I shall not marry her.'

'That is all right; but I expect that it will take *me* all I know to get clear of her. However, there are some occasions in life when one is bound to sacrifice one's own convenience, and this is one of them. After all, she is really very pretty in the evening, so it might have been worse.'

Bottles winced, and Sir Eustace took a cigarette.

'By the way, old fellow,' he said, as he settled himself in his chair again, 'I hope you are not put out with me over this. Believe me, you have no cause to be jealous; she does not care a hang about me, it is only the title and the money. If a fellow who was a lord and had a thousand a year more proposed to her to-morrow she would chuck me up and take him.'

'No; I am not angry with you,' said Bottles; 'you meant kindly, but I am angry with myself. It was not honourable to— in short, play the spy upon a woman's weakness.'

'You are very scrupulous,' yawned Sir Eustace; 'all means are fair to catch a snake. Dear me, I nearly exploded once or twice; it was better than [yawn] any [yawn] play,' and Sir Eustace went to sleep.

Bottles sat still and stared at the fire.

Presently his brother woke up with a start. 'Oh, you are there, are you, Bottles?' (it was the first time he had called him by that name since his return.) 'Odd thing; but do you know that I was dreaming that we were boys again, and trout-fishing in the old Cantlebrook stream. I dreamt that I hooked a big fish, and you were so excited that you jumped right into the river after it—you did once, you remember—and the river swept you away and left me on the bank; most unpleasant dream. Well, good night, old boy. I vote we go down and have some trout-fishing together in the spring. God bless you!'

'Good night,' said Bottles, gazing affectionately after his brother's departing form.

Then he too rose and went to his bedroom. On a table stood a battered old tin despatch-box—the companion of all his wanderings. He opened it and took from it first a little bottle of chloral.

'Ah,' he said, 'I shall want you if I am to sleep again.' Setting the bottle down, he extracted from a dirty envelope one or two letters and a faded photograph. It was the same that used to hang over his bed in his quarters at Maritzburg. These he destroyed, tearing them into small bits with his strong brown fingers.

Then he shut the box and sat down at the table to think, opening the sluice-gates of his mind and letting the sea of misery flow in, as it were.

This, then, was the woman whom he had forgiven and loved and honoured for all these years. This was the end and this the reward of all his devotion and of all his hopes. And he smiled in bitterness of his pain and self-contempt.

What was he to do? Go back to South Africa? He had not the heart for it. Live here? He could not. His existence had been wasted. He had lost his delusion—the beautiful delusion of his life—and he felt as though it would drive him mad, as the man whose shadow left him went mad.

He rose from the chair, opened the window, and looked out. It was a clear frosty night, and the stars shone brightly. For some while he stood looking at them; then he undressed himself. Generally, for he was different to most men, he said his prayers. For years, indeed, he had not missed doing so, any more than he had missed praying Providence in them to watch over and bless his beloved Madeline. But to-night he said no prayers. He could not pray. The three angels, Faith, Hope, and Love, whose whisperings heretofore had been ever in his ears, had taken wing, and left him as he played the eavesdropper behind those blue velvet curtains.

So he swallowed his sleeping-draught and laid himself down to rest.

When Madeline Croston heard the news at a dinner-party on the following evening she was much shocked, and made up her mind to go home early. To this day she tells the story as a frightful warning against the careless use of chloral.

## ABOUT TERRY O'BRIEN

Terry O'Brien is an academic with three decades of experience in teaching language and communication skills in India and abroad. He also headed a college under the auspices of the University of Delhi.

A prolific writer, with several books to his credit, Terry O'Brien is a reputed professional motivational speaker and a quizmaster.